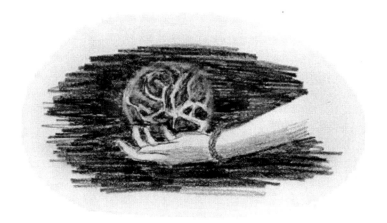

Shadowchild

By C.E. Thornton

Book One of the Guardians of the Light

"Shadowchild"

ISBN 978-0-6151-9044-0

Cover design and photo by C.E. Thornton. Special thanks to Deborah Willson for modeling.

For more information on this book and the author, please visit www.myspace.com/authorcethornton.

To Sean and Shannon, who inspired this story,
And to The Pearl Family,
Who inspire me to live.

Table of Contents

Prologue

Sometimes the weirdest, most unexpected things can happen to you. Many times they take a long time: months, years, before you realize how much you've changed. I guess that my change began long before the part I recall-a part that only took a matter of seconds.

Either way, it seems that change looks to be for the worse, but then you look back and are amazed at how much you've accomplished. At least I was.

That's why I'm writing this.

The events that happened to me may not seem normal-you've probably never heard of the Guardians of the Light, or blue lightning. You probably won't believe this story, but I want to tell it anyway, because you will believe in some of it. Like how in a small number of years, a girl can become a woman.

My name is Benjamina James, and this is my story...

Shadowchild

Chapter One, A Not-So-Little Shock

Bennie James was one of the biggest soccer addicts in all of San Antonio, so anyone who knew her would say. She was always on one team or another, and if she wasn't with friends, in school, eating or sleeping, she was out on the field.

And that hot June day didn't seem to be any different- at first.

Bennie had been at practice for half an hour when the predicted thunder storm rolled in, with blessedly cool air and shade from the hot sun.

It was the cool gusts of wind that attracted Bennie's attention from the drought-yellowed field. She shoved her sweat-dampened bangs out of her eyes to view the charcoal-colored sky, but her eyes fell on a man leaning against the fence around the field. He waved to her.

Who was he?

Bennie knew the occasional parents or bored siblings that would sit and watch someone during practice, but she'd never seen this guy before. She knew for a fact she had met just about every obscure family member of her team mates'. Maybe he was just watching due to lack of anything else to do.

"HEADS UP BENNIE!" came a voice. Bennie's attention snapped back to the field and she saw the ball headed straight for her.

Well, whoever he was, he had an uncanny ability to distract her. Unusual. That could be a problem.

But he wasn't going to distract her now. They had to finish the scrimmage before the storm got too bad and Bennie's focus was entirely on the field.

"Yo, James! Take this one!" Coach Winny's voice called her back, and Bennie lost herself in the game as the sky darkened and the cool rain began to fall in torrents. Bennie sent the ball sailing in a high arc down the field to Amy Gonzales, who took it away to the opposing goal. Bennie risked the temporary pause in her play to glance back at the stands, blinking through the rain.

The small number of people who had come to watch practice were all leaving for the shelter of their cars. But the man still stood there, undaunted by the rain.

He's crazy, Bennie thought as she was called to play offense, dribbling the ball. *But then, I guess we are too, for not stopping even though the lightning could strike any time-*

She'd no sooner had the thought when a white knife of pure electricity came down with blinding force and with a "BRAA-UUM! Buh-boom boom!" struck the sidewalk outside the fence. The entire ground shook dangerously.

"That's it folks!" Bennie heard Coach Winny's voice over the din. "James! Kick it in and we're out of here!"

Damn, I jinxed it. We just got into the zone too. Stupid lightning. Annoyed, Bennie dribbled the ball down the field a little further and gave it a kick…

It flew straight through the air, veering down and to the left, going center… her friend Sarah missed it…

HA! GOAL!!!!!!!!

And then the lightning hit.

All Bennie saw was the glowing electric blue as it came down on her. It touched her on her left shoulder. In the single second Bennie possessed an eternity of thoughts, would it go straight through her, why did it feel like she was growing stronger, painlessly, would it go on? Somehow, she was enjoying this-

-It was over, and Bennie sank into a black calm.

Someone was yelling.

Hmm, I didn't know dying was this cool. Bennie thought…

A thousand faces, all with the same, deep grey eyes. Something red, flaming…sank into her. Bennie looked down but all she saw of her body was a shadow…the voices…the sudden tingling in her shadowy form…

And then a face she'd seen before…but never in person..

Dad?

"What happened? Why isn't she dead?"

"Did you see the color of that lightning? It was *blue!*"

"Blue lightning is actually quite common, if unexplainable. She was lucky it seems to have left her unharmed."

"You think she'll be alright?"

"Definitely, I've seen this happen before. If anything, the sudden charge improves the person's health and performance."

Bennie was hearing all this, and it made sense, but she couldn't, for the life of her, figure out what they were talking about, whoever they were.

She opened her eyes. There was a rather large group-the entire soccer team actually, to her left, all looking shaken, and very wet. Bennie, for the first time, felt every separate drop landing on her face, but her eyes rose to the deep, grey eyes above her.

It was the same man who had been watching them. He was the one who had been giving out information on the blue lightning- that must have been what hit her.

"Good Morning, Bennie." His short, dark beard couldn't hide his smile. Something about it made Bennie smile too, even though she didn't think there was really a matter to smile about. And who told him her name?

"Still morning? How long was I out?"

"All of thirty seconds," The man said. "I'm pretty sure you're ok, but I think Coach Winny here would feel better if we took you up to the hospital for a look." Coach Winny nodded, her blonde ponytail bouncing despite its waterlogged state.

"Thanks, Perce," she said. "I'll call her mom and let her know."

"Shoot," Bennie said. "Maybe you shouldn't. She'll freak out and never let me play outside again. She's always so protective."

The man named Perce laughed. "Everyone feels like that about their mom at some point in their life."

Bennie didn't know why she had to go to the hospital. She'd never felt better, and she checked out just fine, though the lady who checked her out was obviously startled by the reason Bennie was under her microscope.

"Lightning!" the elderly nurse fussed, forcing Bennie into a chair, "You're lucky you're not dead! Never seen anything like this, heard of it, but never seen it... Yes, you called her parents and let them know, sir? Oh, so the coach did." she rambled on some time, having Bennie follow a light with her eyes, stand with her eyes closed, name her birthday, and various other health checks on physical behaviors such as breathing and moving.

The man was talking quietly into his cell phone. He turned around so his right hand, the one holding the phone, was exposed to Bennie's gaze. He had a strange, small tattoo on the base of his middle finger:

$$P^2$$

Bennie somehow sensed it meant something important, though she didn't know why, and could not place it in her mind anywhere.

He hung up the phone, and his hand remained in his pocket. He avoided her eyes. Had he seen her looking at the tattoo?

"Your coach told your mom and she's on her way," he said "She had to get back to the school, but would you like me to wait with you?"

"I think I'm okay, if you need to be somewhere, but if you want to stay you can." Bennie said. Honestly, she wanted him to stay, but only if she could ask him about the lightning, and maybe even about the tattoo on his hand. But she wasn't sure how she would ask him, and she didn't feel that it was a good place to discuss it, with other people around.

"I can stick around," he said, sitting down, "I have the afternoon off."

They didn't say anything for a few minutes, but it wasn't really an awkward silence; it was more like he was waiting for her to start asking questions. Finally Bennie got over her shyness.

"The blue lightning, what exactly causes it?" she asked.

"No one can really answer that," he said slowly, "but it's never hurt anyone- if you're going to get struck by lightning you want it to be the blue kind."

"Do you know what makes it different than normal lightning?" Bennie asked. He shook his head, tucking his jaw-length curly hair behind his ear again.

"In a way, I think it's one of nature's phenomena-one we're not supposed to know about scientifically. It's just- magic I guess."

"You believe in magic?" Bennie suddenly felt like they were going somewhere.

"Do you?" his dark grey eyes twinkled, but their gaze was deep, penetrating-

He had the same eyes as the people in her dream.

Bennie stared back before answering.

"Yes," she said, "I think I do."

Bennie's mom had arrived.

And as Bennie had predicted, her mother was in a panic and said she couldn't believe she'd been allowed out in the rain when there was lightning.

"We were going in, mom! I *promise,*" Bennie said, trying to settle her mom down before she had a heart attack or tried to sue the school. "Coach Winny isn't that stupid."

"I don't think you need to worry," the man said. "A little rest and she'll be right as rain-oh, maybe that wasn't a proper phrase considering the weather."

Bennie laughed, but stopped as her mom looked at him strangely. She seemed to recognize him, or something.

"Oh, mom, this is-uh-"

"My name's Andrew, but everyone calls me Perce," the man said. Bennie thought for a moment about how he could possibly come up with a nickname like that before noticing her mother's suspicious stare.

Uh-oh, not THAT look. Bennie thought. Her mother may have been a small woman but her piercing blue eyes could give even the toughest man the shivers when she gave them The Look.

But her mother surprised her by being very polite.

"Thank you, Perce, for coming along with the coach and keeping an eye on my girl," her mother said, giving her a shoulder hug. "I'll be sure to see to it she doesn't do anything reckless until we're sure she's well."

Perce nodded and shook Bennie's hand and her mother's before making his way through the Emergency Room waiting area towards a young man who looked at Bennie curiously. Bennie had felt Perce put a papery something in her hand and she hid it quickly in her pocket before they left.

Her mother wanted to know every detail of what happened once they were in the car. Bennie replayed it all, but left out the dreams. She was not sure if her mother would think the lightning might have damaged her brain.

"Tell me," her mom said, "Have you spoken to Perseus before?"

"Perseus?" Bennie asked.

"That's what Perce is short for."

"So you *did* recognize him!"

"He was one of your father's friends. I had no idea he was still in San Antonio…"

"Ok, this is just plain weird…" Bennie mused. "And where did the nickname Perseus come from?"

"I don't really know," Bonnie James said, but Bennie knew she was just clamming up again, like she *always* did when it came to things about Bennie's dad. Bennie had to pry before it was too late.

"So you know him and he knows you-how come I've never met him?"

"I don't keep in touch with your father's friends, Benjamina," her mom said with a hardened tone. "They're part of the past and we don't need to relive it, so don't get any ideas."

Bennie tried a little longer to get her mother to say something but it was useless. Her mother never told her anything, and Bennie in return never told her mom anything.

Like the note Perce had handed her. Bennie unfolded the small paper and read it to herself:

```
Bennie,
    I'm pretty sure you have a lot of questions
as to what happened today, but you don't want to
ask them with other people listening. I can tell
you more if you come back to the school courtyard
tomorrow night, after practice. Tell your mom where
you are though. That's always a good idea. ;)
                                        ~Perseus
```

Tell my mom. Bennie smirked. *She'd lock me away and never let me see Perce and ask him anything. She's so paranoid.*

Bennie got out of the car and darted into the house, ignoring her mom. She headed straight for the bathroom. A hot shower sounded very appealing, and it was secluded enough for her to think about the coincidence of Perce being a friend of her dad, who had been killed in an accident when she was just a shadow on the ultrasound.

Not to mention Perce had the same eyes as the people in her dreams.

Bennie shut the door and started the water running, pulling her ponytail out and kicking off her shoes. When she took off her soccer jersey, however, she choked back a startled gasp.

On her left shoulder, where the lightning had hit her, the skin was white, totally devoid of a tan, like she had kept a thick layer of sun block on in the exact same place beside her collarbone, but nowhere else.

The mark was shaped exactly like Perce's tattoo.

Breathing faster than normal, Bennie lifted her gaze up to her eyes-

They're hazel, they've always been hazel…they will be…

They were the exact same deep grey as the people she'd seen in her dream.

Chapter Two, The Guardians of the Light

Blowing off her mother's suspicion by pretending to be going to her best friend Sarah's house, Bennie found herself in the courtyard of Marshall High School that night around nine twenty-five, endlessly pushing her long brown hair back out of her eyes. Questions rolled around in her head.

What does this guy Perce have to do with my parents? What does he know about the lightning, or the mark on my shoulder? How did he know my dad? Heck, what *did he know about my dad? I don't even* know *my dad, thanks to the stupid accident--*

"Hello Bennie," a voice suddenly said. Bennie jumped, and Perce appeared seemingly out of nowhere.

"How did you do that?" Bennie asked.

"We all have our talents," Perce said, grinning wickedly "Including you. Have you noticed them yet?"

"What, the mark and my eyes? And who's we?"

"Well," Perce said, "We have a lot to talk about, you and me. Your mom knows you're here, right?"

"Are you kidding?" Bennie exclaimed. "She would put me in a straight jacket and lock me up, based on her reaction today! What on earth did you *do*?"

"Ahh," Perce said. "I was hoping you were on better terms, but, yeah, I figured she'd probably react this way. We'll work it out though."

"Work what out?" Bennie said.

"Well, Bennie, you may want to sit down because this is going to take a while."

"I hope not too long," Bennie said. "Mom will want me back home before ten and I do need to sleep you know, I have practice tomorrow."

"You don't need sleep, but I'll try not to take too long," Perce said.

Bennie didn't understand that at all but she sat down and kept her mouth shut. Perce wasn't stupid. He knew she was clueless.

"So shoot," she said.

"Firing away," Perce replied. "You remember today, when I asked you if you believed in magic and you said yes?"

Bennie nodded.

"Well, it's good that you believe in it, because it's about to totally weird out your life, but in a good way, I promise."

Bennie said nothing so Perce continued. "That blue lightning is magic, and those it touches are given special powers, spectacular powers. You have magic inside you, Bennie, as did your father, as do I."

"Aha, my dad comes into the picture." Bennie said. "So you, my dad and me all have this magic that makes our eyes grey, so we're all one big happy family?"

"Sort of," Perce said, ignoring the slight skepticism in Bennie's voice. "I'll explain that too. But we should start from the beginning for the best results. Right now I need to tell you where this magic came from, and why we have it, before anything else will make sense. It's no short tale, so I warn you we may be here a while."

"I'll make time," Bennie said.

"Ok, and speaking of time, please just ignore this stopwatch, I'll fit it in for you in a little bit," Perce said, starting up a timer as he began his story:

"In the beginning of time, when the Creator –God you can call him, but universally he has way too many names-made the heavens and the earth, one of his servants turned against him, and evil was born. The Evil One, alias the Devil, and his followers were cast away as demons, and they hid in the darkness. Since then, they have tried to fight their way into power, to gain strength enough to come out of hiding in the shadows. Naturally, God formed a power to fight back, to keep the forces of evil at bay, and to protect the rest of existence. We are but two members of a branch of that positive force. Our branch is called the Guardians of the Light.

"We don't necessarily fight the darkness, but guard the light, as our name suggests. The dark itself is not evil, simply what hides within its depths. The dark is simply a form, the absence of light, with no intelligence or true power. But the fact it can hide things makes it dangerous and often misunderstood as an evil being in itself. We, the Guardians, simply keep the true evil beings weak enough to have to remain hiding. Sometimes we'll join up with or become one of the other forces that fight within the darkness to destroy the sources of evil, but that is not our main job."

"Like offense and defense positions," Bennie said, thinking the allusion was lame but good enough for her.

"Exactly!" Perce said, brightening a bit, and continued.

"As Guardians, each of us has our own powers and abilities, unique to us, though some are similar. Some powers are stronger than others; some are more effective or efficient. Some are even deceiving."

"How are they deceiving?" Bennie asked.

"They may look to be one thing, but really they are another, and some may not seem like a power the forces of good would use. I currently have a young lady in my training–not you, but another whose power lies in seduction. Basically she'll use her wiles to distract enemies into letting down their guard, and then she strikes. Should she touch a being completely with her passionate powers, he would be captivated by her until she released him, and would do whatever she asked to the best of his ability, partly out of desire, partly for freedom. A strange power, but definitely very useful."

"Sounds kind of scary to me," Bennie said. "Almost unethical."

"Yes, but there are a lot of shades of grey in this world," Perce said. "The Guardians figure if God didn't want someone using their power they wouldn't have it, and she's the sweetest girl you'll ever meet. Her name is Gemini, and you'll be meeting her sometime soon probably, as I'm going to be training you too."

"Train?"

"Yes, we'll need to find out what your powers are, and how to use them. I myself am a wizard, so I'm a good instructor; being able to repair any damage done almost instantly." He grinned.

"Is this Guardian business dangerous?" Bennie asked, feigning interest. She had to see how far this joke would go. Perce had to be an actor hired to play her the fool.

When he heard her question, he didn't look her straight in the eye at first.

"Well, it depends," he said. "Everything is dangerous in its own way, but I won't lie to you. Some people would classify us as "superheroes" though it's really not the right word. But all the same, there are "villains" who won't like you getting in their way, which is why you have to be at your best."

"So I guess this is why my mom doesn't want you around, since she knows you're one of these-er-"

"Guardians."

"Yeah, Guardians, and she thinks you'll get me into trouble?"

"She has good reason," Perce said, "But you're only going into training right now and there's nothing saying you *have* to be a Guardian, or even find out what your powers are. But I don't suggest not figuring out how to at least control your abilities, or they might take you by surprise and cause a big mess."

"Yeah," Bennie said. But to herself she was thinking *Guardians? Magic? Mom wants me away from him because he's kooky, not because he's 'just an old friend' of my dad's-*

But Perce was talking again.

"I know, you're thinking 'this guy's a total nutcase, what am I doing here?'"

"What, you're a telepath too?" Bennie remarked, pulling on a mock panic face. Perce burst out laughing.

"No, it's just that I remember what I was thinking when I was told about the Guardians," he said. "I required about five different examples of "proof" before I'd even try to compare what was happening to me with what I was being told."

"Mmmmhhmm," Bennie said, "So this is where the punch-line is, when you tell me to smile for the candid camera?"

Perce grinned.

"No," he said "This is where I point out that I'm going to save you a bit of trouble because I've slowed down time."

"What?" Bennie looked at her watch. It said she had only been gone from the house twelve minutes, when it had taken her ten to walk to the school.

"And now for that stopwatch we've forgotten," Perce said, pointing out that it was still running normally. According to the time on the screen nearly ten minutes had gone by.

"That's trippy!" Bennie said, feeling a perk of excitement when she imagined what she herself might be capable of, if this turned out to be true. Was it so unfeasible after all?

"So, when do I find out what I can do?" she said. Perce laughed again.

"Wow, it took me a lot longer to accept the Guardian speech," he remarked.

Perce walked Bennie to her friend Sarah's house about two blocks away, continuing to talk about the Guardians of the Light, and how the power charged their systems so they didn't need as much sleep as normal people, and could build up to going weeks without a wink. He also talked about the current situations the Guardians were facing.

"Right now, you *really* have to be at your best, because the powers of evil are growing and strengthening like never before," He was saying.

"Why is that?" Bennie asked.

Perce was silent for a moment. The frown on his face was unnerving to Bennie, like seeing someone who lived to solve problems come across one they couldn't remedy.

"That's another part of history which you need to know," he said.

"Do tell."

"About two thousand years ago, the same thing that is happening now, with the evil growing strong, happened. The Guardians could not hold back the forces breaking from the depths of the night.

"But just when all hope seemed lost, a young Guardian emerged with a power no Guardian had ever possessed. With a simple utterance of a phrase she could turn the hearts of the very demons, and they would abandon war for peace, bloodshed for life, hate for love. A phenomenal power she had, to say the least.

"Sounds pretty powerful," Bennie said. "What was her name?"

"Her name was Sheyneh," Perce said. "And she was very powerful.

"Sheyneh's other power was quite interesting. She was a shape shifter, but she could only transform into one thing, a powerful red bird, and from her wings came a fire the color of garnets, which could consume or heal, and with her song she released the power she possessed in its fullest form.

"Sheyneh alone could defeat an entire army, without so much as flying within the shooting distance of an arrow. To the forces of evil she was known only as "The Scarlet Wings" and became their most feared foe."

"The scarlet bird with the flames sounds kind of like a phoenix to me," Bennie said.

"Some believe that's how the phoenix originated in truth, but the only part of her that was immortal was her greatest power, which was named after her. She passed on the Sheyneh- as it is called- to her daughter who was also a Guardian before she herself died, and since then it has been passed to only the most trusted Guardians of that line, waiting for her truest heir to return and take up the power to use."

"Why can't the other Guardians use it?" Bennie asked, "Why only the truest heir?"

"It can be used to an extent, but the full knowledge of the power is only known to the one the power truly belongs to, so only they can use it fully."

"Why is that?" Bennie asked.

"Well," Perce looked thoughtful, "partly because if the Guardians could use it whenever they wanted they would use it so much that evil would be able to grasp its concept and counter it, and also, it can only be used by the one with the heart of Sheyneh because should it be available to anyone, it would have long since fallen into the wrong hands and destroyed us."

"How do you know?"

"Bennie, do you have any idea how the forces of evil have grown so strong?"

"Well," Bennie thought, "Strength comes in numbers, but numbers can only be formed for power through unity-"

"*Exactly,*" Perce said, "Unity. One being has united all the forces of evil, and used much deception to make his numbers grow. He is the King of Darkness-er- the forces under the darkness- and his name is Reyortsed, or so he calls himself. I don't think many people know what his true name is anymore."

"Reyortsed," Bennie repeated. "He's deceived people into becoming his minions?"

"Yes," Perce said. "He's particularly good at convincing people not only because he has astounding power in that area, but he also happens to be a direct descendant of Sheyneh."

"You're not serious."

"Reyortsed simply explains to people his heritage–those who know it–and they believe he's really bringing together a power to destroy evil from the inside-out. We've lost many young, ignorant Guardians to him. They don't know how to fight his persuasive magic, or even detect it. He's as seductive as our Gemini will be when she's ready."

"How do you know that he's really not destroying evil from within?"

"He was never a true member of the Light himself. He never even began the real training. So he has no purpose in doing such an act, and he's also fulfilling a prophecy about Sheyneh."

"What prophecy?"

Perce closed his eyes and recited:

"And a son of Sheyneh shall be stolen away,
Leading many astray as his own,

And the wings of scarlet shall rise once again
To claim his abandoned throne.

"That's part of it anyways," Perce said.

"Does "abandoned throne," mean the power she passed on?" Bennie asked.

"It does," Perce said, "Like I said the power was passed on to Sheyneh's daughter, and the daughter passed it on to her son; it continued through the family that way, though none really knew about it until the previous member of the clan died and they transferred it. Hence Reyortsed knew nothing of the Sheyneh, which would more than likely have been passed to him had he become a full Guardian, as he was powerful and at that time considered trustworthy. But when he turned seeking power of his own the last one to possess it passed it on instead to his nephew, but should that power fall to Reyortsed and had he been able to use it, the world as we know it would be destroyed."

"Does Reyortsed know of this power he should have carried now?"

"Sadly, yes," Perce said, "But he doesn't know who has it now, since at the time of his nephew's death, there was no biological heir of his to take the Sheyneh."

"So who has it now?" Bennie asked, but Perce shrugged.

"Whoever has it never told anyone, but that's probably a good thing. You don't just tell someone you have the greatest weapon against evil in your grasp.

"I think that's all the important things. But we have to talk about your training and your–er– 'classmates'–" Perce grinned.

"But I have one more question, kind of silly, but still I'm curious." Bennie said as Sarah's house came into view.

"What is it?"

"Why did my eyes change color?" Bennie asked. "They were a hazel color this morning but when I got home they were the same color as yours, my dad's and all the people I saw in the dream I had after the lightning."

"Oh! The people you saw in your dream were just other Guardians you've probably met or are related to, like your dad. I knew him, he was a cool guy."

"Thanks." Bennie smiled. "You'll need to tell me more about him sometime."

"You have my word. As for the eye color, I guess it's either a side effect of the magic getting…I guess you could say zapped…into you. Either that or it's just a distinguishing mark of the Guardians."

"Like your tattoo?"

Perce looked startled.

"My tattoo?"

"That mark you have on your hand. The place the lightning touched me- my shoulder, has the same mark." Bennie pulled the neck of her shirt to the side to reveal the top of the mark. She was rather unsettled to see that Perce looked rather awed by the mark.

"That," he said, "Is something we'll have to talk about later, but now is not that time."

Bennie wanted to protest, but something held her back. She trusted Perce, even though she'd only known him about a day. He knew what he was doing.

"But I *will* tell you." He said. Bennie nodded.

"Now, as for your training, I meet in here almost every night around nine-thirty to about two in the morning. My other students aren't here because I had to talk to you, but you'll be meeting them soon, and working with them as well as alone with me.

"I was thinking you could come at the same time tomorrow to meet them and so we could touch in on your mind and see what powers you have, and see if we could discover your Night Name."

"Night Name?"

"Did you really think my friends just nicknamed me after a Greek Warrior?"

"No, I guess not, but what are Night Names?"

"Night Names are the names we go by when we're "on duty" as Guardians. Every person's name reflects their personality, history, or power. Some people find theirs out as soon as they find out what their powers are. Like Gemini; we tease her because her Night Name and her given name are the same thing. I'm called Perseus because I do a lot of fighting-strenuous fighting-and I'm not always cautious about it. That's why I've been made a teacher, to try to push some common sense into me, and some guts into the 'kids'."

"How many students do you have?"

"Just three, now, when including you."

"So who's the third student? There's me and Gemini, who else?"

"Sean," Perce grinned, "My partner in pranks. He's a shape shifter, something like Sheyneh, but still not the same. He can transform into this strange gargoyle-like thing, and into a cat, so he's pretty intimidating and pretty sneaky. He's currently learning how to become a werewolf. His night name is Hadrian. I'll let them tell you more about themselves because they can tell it better than me, and would be annoyed if I told you everything anyway. But that will have to wait for tomorrow night. We're at your friend's house now.

"So we are," Bennie said, ringing the doorbell.

"Well, good night Bennie," Perce said. "I hope your questions are satisfactorily answered, for now at least."

And Perce turned as if to walk away, but instead he dissolved into thin air.

Chapter Three, Classmates and Night Names

Bennie rushed into the courtyard a little late the next night. She had had to wait by her mother's bedroom door for half an hour before hearing her mother's gentle snores above the TV she kept running to help her sleep. Bennie had left a bundle of bedding under her blankets so if her mom woke up and checked on her she'd not find the bed 'empty.' Hopefully she would be too sleepy to wonder why her daughter was under the covers on a hot summer night, air conditioning or no.

But when Bennie arrived at the school it was empty. Maybe Perce had given up on her?

"Hello? Perce?" She called out, immediately wishing she hadn't. What if something bad had happened? From what Perce had told her this whole Guardian business was a bit chancy, and with her callout she'd just announced to anyone who might be lurking around that she had arrived.

Suddenly something huge came swooping down into the courtyard. It had huge, bat-like wings, and its scaly feet and knobbly fingers had long, sharp talons. Small, sharp horns hooked out from its elbows and its head and its body had bear-like brown fur. Huge serrated teeth were bared as the creature roared at Bennie and landed right in front of her.

It was a fortunate thing Bennie wasn't easily frightened- not to mention she had an idea of what the thing confronting her was- or rather *who*, thanks to what Perce had told her.

Suddenly the wizard materialized beside Bennie, confirming her suspicion.

"Sea-an!" Perce rolled his eyes, and the monster suddenly shrank down into the same boy Bennie had seen Perce talking to in the ER. He was doubling over with laughter.

"I couldn't help it! You should have seen her face! She wasn't even scared, just like 'What the heck?'" Sean took a deep breath and calmed himself down, looking at Bennie. "At least we won't have trouble with you scaring at the slightest thing!"

Bennie just raised an eyebrow at Perce, who was losing a battle with himself about not smiling. Finally he cracked too and Bennie just grinned at the two nutcases she had found herself partnered with.

Bennie studied Sean closer, now that he was identifiably human. He had to be at least nineteen. He was pretty tall, about six-foot four, and he wore his light brown hair in a small ponytail in the back, though it still fell in his face in the front.

"Oh goodness me, are they bothering you?" A female voice said, and a tall, mystical figure arrived in a bright glow. The girl who was obviously Gemini sat gracefully on a bench in the courtyard.

"Aww Gem! You missed all the fun!" Sean said, gaining a disapproving glare from the girl.

Bennie was slightly in awe of Gemini, even though Perce had mentioned she was a seductress of sorts. Bennie just hadn't realized that meant "drop-dead gorgeous"-*literally*. Gemini wore a glittering, silvery gown that slid naughtily off her shoulders. Her long hair was completely white, silky and flowing like a unicorn's mane, and her eyes, though the same grey as everyone else's, were large, almost almond shaped, and seemed to glow with a cold fire in her radiant face.

Gemini stood and glided towards Bennie, and instantly her beyond-human beauty vanished. Instead a young woman with shorter, deep auburn hair garbed in jeans and a tank top was coming to greet her. She was still beyond beautiful, even if she didn't look like something out of a fantasy movie.

She was smiling at Bennie.

"I hope you're saner than they are," she said, "I could use someone relatively normal in this posse to keep me from losing all my common sense. Gemini Dean."

"Bennie James." Bennie shook her extended hand.

"And *I*," Sean said with an elaborate bow, "Am Sir Sean Franklin!" He kissed her hand before turning to Gemini.

"And darling Gemini! My lovely gem!" he threw on a corny British accent, "How is the goddess today?"

"Half goddess you mean, *Sir Sean.* And I was particularly well today until I was exposed to your madness!"

"Okay, enough of you lovebirds' playful banter!" Perce said.

"We're not in love!" Gemini said rather forcefully.

"Speak for yourself!" Sean said, throwing on a mock indignant tone. Gemini slid past him and looked at Bennie.

"They're both insane," she warned her. "Try to save yourself from them!"

Then she winked.

"Well, she can't do that until she knows what powers she has, and to do that you need to step away from her so I can help." Perce said, gently pulling Gemini away and purposefully landing her right next to Sean. "Now isn't this a nice spot?"

"Oh wonderful, *exactly* where I'd have chosen, Perce." Gemini rolled her eyes, and Sean gave her a puppy face.

"Doesn't work on her; she's mean!" Perce said to Sean. Gemini made a 'mean' face and Bennie laughed. It was impossible for Gemini to really look malicious.

"Okay, Bennie," Perce said, "First we're going to find out what your powers are and perhaps your Night Name as well. But in order for me to do that, I have to get inside your mind. What I'm going to do is have you sit down —yeah right there's fine- and listen to these two talk about themselves. You won't even know I'm there."

"I don't really like that, not knowing you're there. How am I supposed to tell if someone breaks into my mind?"

"You're sharp," Perce smiled. "But don't worry. We'll train your mind to detect invaders —as well as how to probe others' if ever you needed to-although that's later in training. Defense first. But we have to know what you'll be using to do either."

Perce sat down and closed his eyes as if in meditation, and Bennie sat back and listened to Gemini and Sean tell their stories, which were as interesting as they were. Sean had been a normal kid like Bennie until lightning hit him as well a little less than two years earlier. After that he was petting his cat and wondering what it was like to be one, and then he *was* one. Since then he had learned how to transform into the monster he had so graciously demonstrated for Bennie ("I'm surprised you didn't turn around and go straight home!" Gemini said.), and was currently learning how to shift into a werewolf so he could communicate with other werewolves-not only to protect people from the dangerous creatures, but also to gain their trust for the side of Light. His night name was Hadrian, like the Roman Emperor.

"I guess it's supposed to mean I'm a protector," Sean told her. "I've already seen my share of combat and since I was still a rookie all I really could do was keep watch over my charge."

Bennie noticed Gemini smiled at Sean when he said this. It wasn't a sarcastic or humorous smile, and when Sean noticed his ears turned pink.

They quickly changed the subject to Gemini, who had never been "normal" ("and I cannot say Sean ever really was," she added, over his own protests.). And she wasn't in any part human as far as she knew. Her mother was an elf, and her father was a "god," but not the kind of god Bennie would think of. Gods and goddesses "Are really quite like fairies, though they were taller and didn't need wings for flying." They were beautiful and naturally immortal, but could be killed by poison or severe injuries. Their powers often included artistic creations, music magic, and seduction powers like Gemini's. She was rather fond of her music skills, which were the source of her powers.

"I never knew about Elves and goddesses walking around right here in San Antonio." Bennie said, "Why do you guys insist on being hidden and considered fictional?"

"Partly because there aren't as many of us as there are humans," Gemini said, "So it's easier for our minority to blend, especially since we really never are here. We don't live in this world, and should humans know about us, they'd probably take advantage of our magic qualities. Humans aren't weak you know, rather their lack of magic has given rise to their high-if destructive-intelligence. It's better for us if we keep to ourselves, so humans can advance and we can be happy."

"Hmph, if you can call what we're doing "advancing." Bennie muttered under her breath.

"Ok!" Perce suddenly seemed to come back to life. "You're an interesting character, Bennie."

"I hope you mean that in a good way." Bennie said, wondering what Perce may have been doing inside her head.

"I do. I mean, first I took a look at the dream you had after the lightning hit you, then I moved to where I felt the magic-netic pull-"

"Perce! Why do you make up nonsense words, you dweeb!" Sean said.

"Oh! Dweeb you say to my words, Mr. Werecoyle?"

Bennie looked at Gemini, clueless.

"That's something Sean called himself when he found out he'd be becoming a werewolf next, because he can change into a cat, a gargoyle, and soon a werewolf."

"Ahh," Bennie said.

"Now, no more interruptions!" Perce grinned. "So I followed the pull and found the source of your power."

When he didn't continue Bennie said, "Which is?"

"Bennie, have you noticed anything different about your hands?"

Bennie looked down at her hands. "I...stopped biting my nails?"

"Lift up your arm and aim at the wall."

"Which one?"

"Either-no-Both!" Perce suddenly waved his hands, and the four of them all seemed to be surrounded by a protective force. Bennie lifted her arms.

"Now relax...Feel anything?" Perce asked.

"Yeah..." Bennie *did* feel something, running down into her hands, one was almost cold, tingly, the other a blaze-

"Well let it go then!" Perce said.

Bennie didn't know how she knew just what to do, but she relaxed her body even more and pushed with her arms.

Suddenly an eruption of flames burst out of her left hand, not burning her, just flying freely away as if she wasn't the source.

"Holy--!" Bennie never finished what she was about to say because a second later something blindingly white and jagged came charging out of her other palm-

Lightning!

"Pull it back, Bennie!" Perce shouted.

Bennie tensed up, and she felt the power pull back and away into her, knocking her flat on the ground.

"Damn," was all she could say as Perce released the shields he'd placed on them for protection. With a wave of his hand the chars from the fire and the hole she'd blasted almost completely through the brick wall of the cafeteria were gone.

"Strong language, but not as strong as what I was thinking!" Sean remarked.

"And that's not all," Perce said.

"I don't think I want any more surprises tonight, Perce."

"Trust me, it's too cool to miss, but it won't make the school look like it was a terrorist target. Ok so that wasn't funny, but trust me!"

"What else can I do, transform my hair into wire and bind someone up in it?" Bennie was still getting used to the fact she could blow the school roof away simply by raising her hand in class.

"No, but I did once work with a young lady who could do just that!" Perce winked. "You remember when in your dream you looked down at yourself and saw only shadow?"

"Yeah," Bennie found it strange for someone she hadn't even told that to telling her about it like he'd dreamed it too.

"Let's step into the shadows, shall we?" Perce led Bennie over to a particularly dark corner. Bennie had just stepped out of the light when Gemini blinked curiously and Sean said "Hey, where'd she go?"

"I'm right here!" Bennie said, but when she finally realized the two of them really couldn't see her, she tried to look at herself only to find she wasn't there at all.

"Perce-"

"Bennie this is got to be the most fascinating power I've seen in years, and that's saying something. You use Evil's own weapon against them."

Perce blacked out the courtyard with a wave of his hand. "Can you see anything?"

Bennie noticed that she could see something-*everything* in fact. Even though she was standing in darkness, it was as if the sun had come up to her eyes.

"You're the essence of Darkness, Bennie," Perce said as he turned the lights back on, "But you carry the extremes of light inside you."

They stepped back out into the light, Bennie visible again.

"So you're saying I can't be seen, but can see, in the darkness?"

"Yup."

"And then I use the lightning and fire to strike?"

"That's what I'm saying."

"Cool!" Bennie, Sean and Gemini all said at the same time.

"I'll say!" Perce said.

"So did you figure out my Night Name?" Bennie asked. Perce looked slightly troubled.

"Not everyone's is that easy to find, some people go for years without knowing theirs, others never find out at all. But I think for now, we can call you Shadowchild. You're basically a shadow-"

"Not to mention the youngest one here-" Sean noted.

"Sean! You're what? Three years older than her?" Gemini swatted Sean on the arm. He just grinned. "She made physical contact with me!"

"I'll make more than that if you don't hush!" Gemini began to glow menacingly, but Bennie ignored them.

"Shadowchild," She said the name again. It sounded cool, but somehow not totally fitting.

But then it wasn't her real Night Name. That would be harder to find.

She looked up at Perce and smiled with a shrug.

"It works for me."

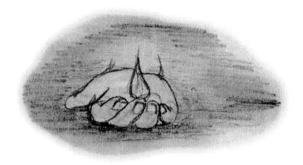

Chapter Four, Sensitive Powers

Bennie crept into her house quietly later that night. She went in through her bedroom window so she wouldn't wake her mom. Her hands felt slightly hot after her first lessons on training the fire and lighting to go in the right direction. More than once Sean had turned into a gargoyle again so he could grab Gemini and fly them out of the way. He seemed to enjoy it very much but Gemini always seemed quite annoyed, and protested she could move herself, thank you very much. Bennie got the idea Gemini and Sean had always had this type of relationship.

A floorboard creaked under Bennie's foot and she winced. That would surely wake everyone up.

But then she realized she did not remember that floorboard creaking before, not noticeably anyway. She took another step toward her room.

Once again, the sound seemed keener.

I guess it's only natural for my hearing to be sharper, like my eyes in the dark, now I'm changed, Bennie thought.

She wondered if she was going to be able to get used to this. Something made her uncomfortable: a feeling she was going in over her head. But could she refuse? Could she say no to what she was? Could she deny the fact she was no longer just Bennie James?

No, she supposed she could not. But did that mean she had to use the powers she had?

If my father did, then I should too. I just hope I'm right.

Bennie decided that even if she needed sleep she could not have slept if she wanted to. She paced about restlessly until dawn.

"You alright Bennie?" Bennie's friend Sarah came to sit by her as she ate after practice several days later. "You seem, preoccupied. I notice you keep looking at your hands out there on the field."

Bennie chewed her apple hard. Since her training had begun, it had become harder to push the power back down. The strange stinging combined with trying not to set the field on fire when she stopped a goal normally would have distracted her badly, but then, Bennie was not normal anymore. She did not enjoy having something like that to hide.

"Just, the new lotion I tried makes my hands feel funny," Bennie lied.

"Can I see?" Sarah asked. She was always trying to figure out strange things like these. Bennie had no choice but to humor her. She held her hand out to Sarah.

"Just feels like skin, so it must be your imagination," Sarah said, "What lotion did you use?"

"Uh," Bennie thought fast. "A--sample that came in the mail. Don't remember the name."

"Oh, those can be really cool sometimes, but I once got one and it smelled awful!"

Bennie nodded absently. She hated lying, especially to her friends. It never got her anywhere but stressed.

She felt eyes on the back of her neck. She turned around.

An orange cat was sitting on the fence, watching her. It winked.

Sean!

"Who's cat is that?" Sarah had turned around too.

"I'm not sure. Here kitty!" Bennie teased. The cat that was Sean flicked his tail as if to say, "You wish!"

"Oh come on, little one!" Bennie said in baby talk as she walked slowly over to the snobby cat and picked him up before he could get away. Green eyes gave her a look that spoke purely of revenge.

Sarah, however, was oblivious to Sean's sinister thoughts and started stroking him endlessly. Sean put on a rather convincing show as 'the cute little kitty' by purring loudly, lifting up his chin for a scratch, and trying to coax Sarah into giving him some of her tuna sandwich by rubbing against her legs. He succeeded.

It was all Bennie could do not to laugh.

Later that night Gemini had to bring Bennie down from the roof. Sean had turned into his gargoyle self again and made Bennie play pet, and proceeded to forget to let her down. Sean was currently working in the corner with Perce on becoming a werewolf. He was having more trouble than usual because physical contact with whatever he was trying to transform into seemed to be a key in his prior success.

"With the cat it was instantaneous ability, and the gargoyle wasn't too hard because I just imagined it up myself," Sean said as he tried to think away the fur he had managed to grow. Gemini just glanced up from where she was composing some music. Perce had charmed a bubble around her so the rest of them would not hear the sound and be distracted. Bennie tried to focus on reducing the fire charge from her hand. No matter what she did, a bonfire always came out instead of a single little flame.

"Is learning magic like this always this frustrating?" Bennie said exasperatedly as Perce quenched the flames in the trees across the courtyard. "I mean, it not only blasts every time, it goes every which way!"

Perce grinned. "Your abilities might be powered by emotions, so depending on your stress level, or whether you're happy or angry, it may be affected. That's what happened to me. You should have seen me when I was learning levitation and telekinesis. I kept lifting the wrong things, including something I wouldn't ever mention for fear of blackmail."

"I've been trying to figure out what it was since I first heard of it," Sean said through unusually sharp teeth, "He apparently had a rather interesting time of it trying to get where he is now, with his 'skills.'"

"The point is," Perce interjected quickly, but Bennie didn't miss the change of color in his face. "Yes, it is frustrating. It would be less so if everyone had similar powers, but that would also be boring. We'd all end up in big classrooms with big books full of the same things, just like regular school, though I hate to contaminate the last of summer with the word."

"You're telling me! I go into AP English next year!" Bennie shuddered, thinking guiltily of the remaining book and essay she still had to do in preparation. "English is one of my better subjects, yeah, but where am I going to find time to do this, play soccer, eat, do my homework, and also sleep-oh wait never mind."

Gemini laughed. "That's an advantage of being a Guardian: You don't need so much sleep! You can pull all-nighters without trouble, and also have training time."

"Haha! Yeah, but anyway, backtrack from the digression." Perce never lost his train of thought entirely. "It really makes you feel more triumphant in the end when you learn to control the powers all by yourself. Some people can be helped, like I was, because at the time a rather nice mage was my instructor. He knew what I was trying to do, which was saying something. *I* didn't even know what I was trying to do! He could throw fire too, like you do."

"Is he still around?" Bennie asked. Maybe he could help her keep from burning down the whole school.

"Heavens no, he was in his seventies then, had been a guardian for more than fifty of those years, unusually long time for anyone. Even the immortals usually leave-for a little while at least. At the moment we have most everyone on task though. But anyway, Mr. Edwards as we called him retired. He was chilling out with his wife in the Hill Country actually, but he was tracked down by an old enemy," Perce scowled. "Cowardly, taking an old man by surprise when he was just starting to relax."

Bennie looked down at her hands awkwardly, "Who was the enemy?"

"It doesn't matter now," Perce said, "He never made it out of there alive. Mr. Edwards' friends made sure of that."

Chapter Five, Fear and Fighting

Bennie's feet paced her bedroom floor nervously as she sleeplessly passed the rest of the night. For once she wished sleep was necessary to the Guardians because she wanted to escape the uneasy feeling that was growing inside her.

Something about the way Perce had told her his enemy had never made it from the house alive had disconcerted her. She understood there were dangers involved in this Guardian job, but she also understood a Guardian had to have been there that night, and had gotten there too late to save their friend, but in time to kill the killer.

Bennie knew Perce had done it. It was obvious. But the fact he had killed someone gave Bennie a view to the truth she had not totally comprehended. Perce was dangerous. The Guardians were dangerous. *She* was dangerous. She could kill.

Bennie didn't want to kill anyone. She looked down at her palms. They looked perfectly normal. But when she pictured what they could do to a living thing she was suddenly terrified of herself.

She did not want this. She did not need this.

Her arm grew hot.

"Oh shit," she said out loud trying to pull back the flames before they erupted and consumed the house. Her terror increased as she sped toward the window to eject the danger into the darkness.

Only a tiny flame-a candle flame, appeared. Bennie warily drew back her arm.

She looked at the small flame, and it comforted her. She was not always dangerous after all. She could be as gentle and calm as a small candle in a dark room.

The flame went out. Bennie wondered why as the power receded from her arm. She had not called it back.

Then she understood.

She had been frightened by what would happen if the flames were too big. That fear had controlled how much fire had appeared. When she had calmed down, satisfied with what she had seen, the flames had ceased. Her power was triggered by emotion! Only what she felt controlled what happened in regards to her magic. That was the key.

She wondered if Perce was by any chance still at the school, so she could tell him. She had nothing else to do, after all. Besides, not only was this something to talk about, she wanted to know the truth about killing and fighting in this business.

She went out quietly.

Bennie did not live far from the school, but her mother still would have killed her for walking there in the dead of night, so she left a bundle of blankets in the bed to look like she was still there. Bennie really could have cared less at the moment if her mom knew or not. She had other things on her mind, so naturally she did not notice someone was following her.

Bennie rounded a bend in the road. She could see the school from here. But she paused because someone was standing in her way. She looked up, but was shocked to find she could not focus on the person's face. It was as if her eyes were looking through it. She blinked.

"Don't bother trying," A voice that Bennie did not like echoed from the faceless being. It sounded feminine, but not human. Bennie already sensed the presence of someone behind her.

"Try what?" Bennie said, thinking more and more this was positively the worst thing that could have happened right now.

"*Anything,*" said a deep growl from behind Bennie, even less appealing to her than the voice of the faceless creature. Fear prickled up Bennie's spine. She carefully turned around to see what the other monstrosity was. As soon as she did she wished she had left it at the creature's voice.

All she could see was a hunched, scrawny silhouette. The creature seemed to absorb all the light around it. When Bennie's magically enhanced eyes adjusted to seeing why, she screamed in horror at it as her sight went completely black.

They dropped something on me! Bennie thought, then grew confused as she felt nothing over her head when she reached to pull the blackness off. She realized with shock she was blind.

No, I'd say that was probably even worse than getting here in the first place? Bennie thought frantically. She could hear her breathing raggedly leaving her chest as her attackers laughed.

"She's obviously not used to the ways of our world," The womanlike creature said as she grabbed at Bennie's arm.

Bennie jumped back, trying to move away from the two. It wasn't easy as she couldn't see where they were and they were being very quiet. She could not even try to find a shadow to hide in because she could not see where she was going.

I'm going to have to burn them down. I have to kill them. I can't!.

No, she had to kill them. She wouldn't go with them, and she could not let them escape since they would know where to find her, and how to fight her. Actually they already did, it seemed, when she was able to focus her mind on what the female voice was saying.

"This one has interesting powers, Gregk," she said smoothly, "Her eyes penetrate pure darkness, unusual for a Guardian."

"Perhaps she is not one of them," the creature called Gregk said, "Perhaps she is one of the *others.*"

"I doubt that. They don't walk where we can see them. They're not so foolish."

"Where *you* can at least. The light is pointless with me."

Bennie felt the heat carrying through her hand. She had to kill them now. In a rage she leapt up and released what she hoped was a huge fireball in the direction of the voices.

She heard a loud, rending screech and smelled something burn, but it was not flesh. The fumes of whatever it was choked her. She blacked out as she heard loud incantations from more than one voice...

Bennie opened her eyes but only darkness greeted her. Panic flooded her mind. The blindness had remained. Where was she? Was anyone else there? Who? Had the flames worked? How long had she been out?

"She's awake," someone said. Bennie felt someone touch her. She screamed.

"Whoa! Whoa! Calm down Bennie, you're okay, you're okay," someone was saying. Bennie stopped struggling against Perce's arms.

"It's me," Perce said soothingly. But Bennie was cautious, drawing lightning into her hand.

"How do I know it is you?" She snarled, her blind eyes fluttering about. At least she could control them. It was just the impenetrable darkness...she hated it.

"Shh, *nesenta,*" Perce said, and Bennie began to calm down. The word meant something, but she did not know what. She knew it was him now, though. Her heart slowed and the electricity in her arm began to subside.

"Perce, what happened? Why can't I see?"

"I don't know," Perce said, sitting Bennie up on the soft ground. Bennie realized she was on a bed.

"But why am I here?" She asked, shaking no matter what she did to try and stop.

"I came to check on you last night because I noticed you seemed disquieted," Perce said. "I got there in time to see you throw what looked like a nuclear bomb at this walking black hole. You sure took care of that one!"

Perce said this almost proudly as he supported Bennie with a hand on her shoulder. Bennie felt a spark in her chest.

"What about the other one?" she asked flatly.

"She protected herself with a firewall but I brought her down. She's in the custody of the Guardians right now."

Bennie started shaking. She shut her eyes against the tears that were coming.

"Perce, I killed someone. I *killed* them." She stuttered as she spoke again, "You're acting like it's a happy matter to be proud of!"

"You aren't afraid to defend yourself!" Perce said in an attempt to calm her. It failed.

Bennie shook his hand from her shoulder and jumped up to find her way to the door. She collapsed weakly on the floor.

"Bennie!" Perce tried to help her.

"GET AWAY! WHAT ARE YOU TRYING TO DO TO ME!?!?!" She screamed, crawling away. "SCARE ME INTO TAKING PEOPLE OUT FOR YOU?"

"No, Bennie, listen to me!" Perce sounded almost as frantic as Bennie felt. "I didn't mean it like that."

Bennie kept struggling away, but she gave up and sat on the floor. She felt Perce sit beside her.

"I don't believe in killing!" Bennie said hoarsely. "What happens to anyone who leaves people they love behind? Would you like it if someone killed someone close to you?"

Perce was silent for a long time. Guiltily Bennie knew someone had killed a close friend of his-his teacher.

"Bennie, the first time is always terrible. It's never easy to kill, never. But you were defending yourself. You did what you had to instead of lying there panicked. Maybe it's not right to kill, but had you refused, they'd have done worse to you before letting you die. You have to know that. I mean, look at it this way. You were struck blind by something no one has ever been able to see, and you still had enough sense to try to take out the danger even when the odds were against you. You've gone that far in only a few days, and faced a danger most Guardians don't come to for years after they are formed. You have fear, but you don't let it control you. That's why I'm proud of you."

Bennie leaned into his arms, blind eyes full overflowing with tears.

"I would never have wanted you to face killing so soon, Bennie..." Perce spoke pleadingly. "I never dreamed I would have to do that at your age, and I'm a macho guy who loved blowing up Space Invaders at the arcade as a kid."

Bennie took a shuddering breath.

"Killing wasn't hard when you killed your teacher's enemy, though, was it?" she prodded.

She could tell Perce was smiling.

"Perception is a good trait too. And no, it was very hard to kill him."

"Why?" Bennie said, turning towards Perce.

"Because I don't kill unless I have to, especially not people I was friends with," Perce said.

Bennie turned her face to him, but was frustrated that she couldn't look at him.

"You'd be surprised to know that I've only ever killed three people in all the years I've been a Guardian. Most people have bloodier records."

"Why is that?" Bennie said, "What makes it different for you?"

"I can personally relate to the families of those who are killed," Perce said, and Bennie felt him gently lift her up and carry her back to the bed. She lay back on the pillows, feeling very helpless.

"My eyes-- Will I get my eyesight back?"

Perce sighed and sat down on the edge of the bed.

"I don't know, Bennie. We've called in the healers, and it's all up to them and to you."

Healers? Bennie thought. *That's not a common term.*

"Perce, where are we anyway?"

"Safe, Bennie," he said quietly, "That's all you need to think about right now, you'll be too curious if I try to explain where we are. I'm going to put you to sleep so you can relax, and we'll get you home before morning."

Bennie agreed that was wise. After all, she had wanted to sleep earlier that night before she went to find Perce.

It's still the same night. Now it may never end for me.

Chapter Six, Aila

Bennie awoke, her eyes still covered by complete blackness. It took her a moment to remember what had happened.

She fleetingly thought maybe this was all she would ever see again, all because she had looked at that stupid-stupid-

Panic jerked her out of her reverie. She *had* to get her eyesight back. She would get it back. She couldn't do this, going on without it, and how would she explain her sudden blindness to her friends, or worse, her mom?

She'd lock me away and never let me see Perce again. I'd never get a chance to figure out what this is all about.

Bennie shuddered. She could hardly think about thinking about it, having these abilities and never knowing what they were, and never being able to see again, for that matter. That on top of the fact that she had killed the thing that had caused all this only made her feel worse, but why she did not know. After all, it deserved it, and she was only protecting herself.

Never mind, she thought, *You don't like killing, and you'll just have to live with the fact that you did.*

Bennie's thoughts were interrupted by the sound of a door opening.

"Who's there?" She spun toward the sound and lifted her hand. A little zap would take care of any enemy, that was for sure.

"Bennie, it's me, and put your hand down!" Sean spoke softly and nervously, "I heard what happened, and I came to see you before Aila arrives."

"Who's Aila?" Bennie asked.

"Aila's a Healer," Sean said, "And a good friend of Perce's. She'll take care of you better than anyone. She's nice, but not a softy."

"What is she going to try?" Bennie said.

"I'm not sure," Sean said. "But with her it'll work, one way or the other."

"Hmm," Bennie said, hoping he was right. Then she realized Perce had never told her where she was, or how long she'd been there, since it had still been the same night when Perce had spoken to her.

Mom will absolutely kill me if she finds I'm gone.

"Sean, where the hell are we anyway? Perce wouldn't say. I think I upset him earlier."

"No, he's not upset because of anything you said, he's upset about what happened," Sean said, "Says it's his fault you're hurt, that as your protector he should have prevented this. He's beating himself up about it right now, saying all he's good at is slowing down time so you'd get an hour of sleep in 6 minutes. He uses that ability so often it makes me wonder what time really is, as a matter of fact…"

"What on earth is he talking about?" Bennie said, exasperated. "If I remember correctly *he* was the one who saved me! He showed up just in time. The fact he knew I was looking for him at all amazes me, never mind being there to get me out of trouble. What is he, a telepath?"

"No, he's not that powerful," Bennie could almost see Sean smiling. "It's just after a wizard goes into someone's mind to find their source of magic, a bit of an empathic connection forms for a while, so he could tell when you wanted to see him. It usually only lasts about an hour or so, but it apparently lasted longer in your case."

"A lot longer," Bennie thought aloud. "Why?"

"Not sure, maybe it's just a fatherly instinct. He's known what I'm thinking more than once, even when he'd barely met me."

The door opened again. Bennie turned toward the sound.

"Hey Aila," Sean said to the newcomer. "Good to see you again."

"And you, Hadrian," the soft voice used his Night Name. Her low tone was as sinister as it was soothing. Sean must have noticed Bennie felt that way. He patted her shoulder.

"She always got me out of a fix when I messed up on my gargoyle transformation. I'll come back when she's finished."

"Why don't you stay?" Bennie could not help but feel a bit apprehensive to be alone with a stranger that she could not see.

"Distraction," the voice named Aila said. "Friends and family can interfere or get distressed, or cause it, so they only come in when it is necessary for healing. He will return when we are ready."

Bennie felt someone's weight added to the bed she was seated on. Whoever she was, Aila was very light, from what Bennie could tell. The sag in the mattress was very slight compared to when Sean had sat down on it.

"Welcome, Shadowchild, you may call me Aila," the voice said. "I am sorry we must meet under these circumstances, but Perce hasn't had a chance to bring you here before now." Bennie felt a small, cool hand come under her chin. "Tilt your head back, yes just like that, so I can see into your eyes."

Bennie felt warmth on her face, as if a beam of light were shining on her. She did not know what to say to this new acquaintance, nor did she know what to think of her. All Bennie could tell was that Aila was not a human, but how Bennie knew she could not tell.

"Odd." Bennie jumped at the sudden pronouncement.

"What's odd?" Bennie said.

"Well, as far as I can see, nothing is wrong with your eyes *physically*," Aila said. "It seems that something spiritual-or emotional- has simply blocked your eyesight, sort of a black shadow over the retina, blocking any images from reaching the photoreceptors. Whatever it was you saw could not have been nice, to put it lightly."

"I can't even bring myself to think about it," Bennie trembled slightly.

"That must be the key, then," Aila said, "It's not physical, it's emotional blindness. The horror has practically settled in your eyes and they are blocking sight in defense of your mind and heart. Until you can bring yourself to face what you saw, your eyes will keep themselves closed."

"Are you sure?" Bennie asked, "I mean, is there nothing you can do?"

"Nothing is certain in this case," Aila said, "The creature you saw has been noted to appear to most as 'clothed in darkness.' No one has ever seen one before. But your eyes, thanks to your power, simply peer through the absence of light as if the sun shone there. You could see it, and your blindness-and your memory, I assume, determine the reason for the creature's mask: it is too evil to be seen.

"As for me being able to do anything, I can only tell you how to see without your eyes at this point. It is up to you to gain back what you had, and that could take some time."

Frustration threatened to surge through Bennie, and she felt her eyes burn with tears, but Aila murmured something Bennie could not hear, and Bennie felt her heartbeat calm again.

Perce pulled that stunt too. He must have learned it from her.

Bennie put the thought aside for a moment and focused on the present situation.

"What can you teach me, then, until I can face what I saw?" Bennie said, and to her surprise, Aila laughed.

"I can't teach you anything you don't already know, Benjamina," she said lightly.

"Then how am I supposed to get on with life?" Bennie said, more confused than frustrated. It was something in Aila's laugh...it was pure as if a five-year-old had just opened a long awaited gift on Christmas.

"Let's put it this way," Aila said. "What can you tell me about me, just based on what you've *observed* in the past few minutes? I am certain you could tell I am no human, couldn't you?"

"How did you know?"

"Even with shadows in your eyes, I can still see your thoughts."

"And I can tell you're smiling, by the way your voice sounds," Bennie said, "I can s-no, not see, but *feel* your shape, and there's something in your voice that's not like a human's, and your hands were smaller-like a child's. But the way you act and talk is much older than that, though I can tell by your weight on the bed your body is proportional to your hands."

"Like I said, you don't even need me to tell you how to see," Aila laughed again, and Bennie felt a prickle of hope. "You know how to use your sense of hearing and your sense of touch to determine my age-and if you knew more about the true races of the universe, you would know that what was not normal about my form is that I have wings, and that I am a fairy."

Bennie heard a fluttering, and felt Aila flying before her, landing gently on the floor.

"You're only about four feet tall, if that," Bennie said.

"Correct again. Now, can you tell where I come from?"

"Pardon?"

"What type of land is my home? Can you tell?"

Bennie thought hard, but couldn't understand how she should know.

"Your sense of smell is not as keen as another creature's, but should you be blind long enough, you would begin to tell in slight measures the scent of the forest, of trees and earth surrounding me, and such. Follow me. We're going to help you adjust to walking in darkness, and get you some sense enhancers.

Bennie slowly and nervously made her way across the room to the door. She bumped her shoulder on the frame slightly as she turned out into the hall, but for the most part was capable of walking straight by reaching out for a wall's guidance occasionally, and mainly by following Aila's light footsteps.

"What are sense enhancers?"

"They're just what their name says they are," Aila said, "It's a set of potions to increase certain senses: smell, touch, hearing. I am going to get you touch and sound enhancers because in your field of work those are the ones you will need most. A touch enhancer can increase your sensitivity to light so much that you can read the pages of a book simply by feeling the difference between the white light reaching your skin and its absence where the letters are printed in black ink. It takes a bit of getting used to at first, but it can make any normal person believe you can see, even if you don't always look them in the eye."

"That's just plain freaky," Bennie had to say.

"You'll find things far stranger in this life, I'm afraid," Aila said. "But we all start with the baby steps right? And I mean that in a good way."

Bennie had to agree with that- as well as stumble into another doorway. She sighed. It had not even been two weeks since she had gained her powers and already they were beginning to seem more annoying than interesting.

She tried to reason with herself that she had had very little experience to prove or disprove that fact, and that it was simply bad luck she had walked right in the path of a–never mind what it was. That she had crossed paths with *it* so early on was unfortunate all around, but she still wished she had just told Perce "no" from the start.

No you don't, and you know it. Bennie won the argument with herself, and grinned. *Wow. I should have joined the debate team,* she thought sarcastically.

Judging by the echoes, Bennie had followed Aila into open air-and it seemed to be full of people, like a city. But the clearest sounds were to her left, and they were of people fighting.

"They're just sparring, not to worry," Aila said. "We're not in a war zone or anything."

"Aila, I don't even know where we are, never mind it being a war zone or not," Bennie said. "Perce never said, and Sean didn't get a chance."

"Ah yes, I forget you've not been here yet. We are in Pelanca, headquarters of the Guardians of the Light."

"Pay-lan-ca?" Bennie's mouth formed around the strange name.

"It's almost an initiation for new Guardians to be brought to Pelanca to see it before they know about it," Aila said, taking Bennie's arm as she got disoriented in all the noise. "But in your case we'll make an exception. This way, sweetheart. That's the street, not the sidewalk."

"So Pelanca is kind of like the capital of Guardian-dom," Bennie said. "Is it a city? Who lives here?"

"Many."

"Well, I would assume that, but I mean what kinds of people?"

"Many."

Bennie laughed. It felt good to. "Are you saying that on purpose?"

"Of course," Aila said, amusement in her voice, "I don't want to say much about the city because it will ruin the effect the city has on you when you first see it."

"Great," Bennie said, her brief moment of joy fading. "I'm really going to be screwed if I can't get my sight back soon."

"You will, Shadowchild," Aila said, her voice calming, "You have the will, and the need."

Chapter Seven, Solace in the Sun and Moon

After Aila had given Bennie the sense enhancers Perce came back to take her home. Just before Bennie took leave of the house in the city she could not see, Aila placed something in her hand. Bennie felt a chain, and something smooth-a stone pendant of sorts-resting comfortingly in her palm.

"I wish I could give you more to help, but this is the best I have," Aila said. "It's a moonstone; the chain is white-gold, to represent the beauty of the Sun and Moon. They were put in the sky to guide us by day and by night, and you must always remember that, Bennie. Remember the Moon and his children, the stars, are always with you, even on the darkest nights, and they will guide you."

Bennie was speechless, and in the end thanked Aila with just a hug. She was already quite attached to the small, wise fairy, despite their short time together.

Bennie took Perce's hand as he led her through the noisy streets. Even with the first dose of sense enhancers already making her 'see' Pelanca in a strange way, she didn't trust herself not to trip or stroll right into a street.

After a quick drive in a silent car, or something like a car, Perce led her into what seemed to be a small cave.

"Perce, where exactly are we going?" Bennie was just beginning to wonder how they were going to get back to San Antonio when Perce held her tight against him and said "We're going home, so hold on!"

"Perce-how are we-GOOD NIGHT SNAKES!" Bennie screamed as they suddenly rocketed upward at a frightening speed.

"PERCE!!!!!!!!!!!!!!!!!" Bennie shouted. After the initial shock of realizing that *Perce* was the one propelling them Bennie had enough emotion left to scold him for not warning her. But soon she was just laughing as the air whooshed past her. Bennie could feel them turning about in what was obviously an elaborate network of tunnels. Left, Right, Half Right, Two lefts, all going slightly up until finally they were going straight up.

Within minutes they were on the surface again-somewhere well away from Pelanca city it seemed, as well as San Antonio.

"Perce, good grief!" Bennie said, panting and laughing as he let go of her and put her own her own two feet..

"Sorry Bennie," Perce said, "I should have warned you, yeah, but it's so much fun to see how people react to flying for the first time!"

"You're a danger to society!" Bennie said, "A danger who can fly too. That's not a good combo, Perce."

"I'm just a troublemaker with a knack for magic-just a bad combo altogether," Perce said, but Bennie heard the grin on his face. "Aila told me once when I ran into a wall when I was first learning to fly that I was going to get myself killed before I turned 35."

"And just how old are you now?"

"Awww no! Don't ask me that!"

"What? Think I'll think you're too old to be a cool teacher?"

"Well…" Perce was grinning, Bennie could tell. "We'll just say I'm three years overdue to get myself killed."

"Works with me," Bennie winked.

"Well to keep us out of more trouble let's get back to the school, and I'll walk you home." Perce reached out and snatched Bennie off the ground again.

"Wait! No! PERCE! NOT SO FAST!" Bennie was beginning to feel dizzy now, but the fresh air helped.

"I have to get you there quickly!" Perce said. "I can't slow time forever, you know, and we're out past Helotes as it is!"

Perce did slow down though, and Bennie was glad of it. She felt close to being sick by the time they landed in the school courtyard.

Bennie realized she had been closing her eyes the whole time. She hadn't been able to tell the difference because of her lack of vision. With a pang she wondered when her eyes would really open again, if ever.

I've been blind for a matter of hours, and I already miss seeing the world so much…

Her spirits sank lower as Perce guided her back to her house. He relinquished his hold on time, grunting as if he'd just thrown a heavy box off his weight.

"Harder than it seems," Perce said. "We've passed seven hours in not even two. All the people sleeping will be really well rested. No need to thank me or anything."

But he stopped his cajoling when he saw that Bennie was in no mood for it.

"You okay, Shadow?" He said, using a new nickname.

"I dunno," Bennie said, "I guess I'm just feeling a little funny."

Perce didn't say anything, he just put his arm around her.

"It's gonna be okay," he said, "Trust me, I'll take care of you."

"Perce…" Bennie said, her voice quivering despite her efforts to sound calm. Perce had been walking her back down the walkway to her door, but he stopped.

"Perce I…" Bennie didn't know how to say what she was feeling. Whenever someone who knew the things she had been through had been near her she had been able to push the sight and fear of *It* from her mind, but now she suddenly felt it overwhelm her, and the darkness her eyes used as a shield grew thicker until it blurred all her senses, and her eyes burned with tears.

Bennie, grow up! Bennie thought at herself. Oh, this sure was brave wasn't it? Crying over something she had killed, over that-

"It's alright Shadow," Perce put his hand on her shoulder, "Come on, I'll walk you in."

He led her in through the back door, casting a silence charm so Bennie's mom wouldn't wake up. He helped her up the stairs and she went into her room quickly and changed.

"Come outside with me for a minute," Perce said when she opened the door again, a little more comfortable in a pair of track pants instead of jeans.

Bennie followed Perce out to the backyard, and he slowly lifted them through the air until they settled on the roof.

"Here, give me your hand," he said softly, turning her palm upward. "You feel that?" He gently stretched her upturned hand out in front of her. Bennie thought she could feel something warm and heavy pressing on her hand and slipping through her fingers. Yet it was almost an imagined feeling.

"What is it?" Bennie asked, tilting her face to the strange feeling. Her senses began to clear, her mind began to calm.

"Wait, and you'll see," Perce almost whispered, a gentle smile in his voice.

And suddenly she *could* see it!

The Moon. She could see the moon. She could *see* it!

"Perce! My eyes!" She spun around to look at him, but she could see no more than she had since she had taken the sense enhancing potion, "Wait…it's gone again."

"Keep looking at the Moon, Bennie. You're not just seeing with your eyes, you're feeling it." Perce wrapped his other arm around her, turning his own head to the sky. "Feel the Moonbeams melt around you, feel them wash your fears away. Nothing else on earth can calm you like Moonbeams or sunlight. Even in darkness they are there somewhere, you just have to find them and let them guide you to the light again."

Bennie breathed slowly and deeply, her heartbeat slowed and the visions behind the black cloak her eyes wore faded in the light of the Moon.

"That sounds like what Aila said," Bennie told him.

"Really?" Perce said, sounding interested.

"Yes, then she gave me this." Bennie heard Perce breathe a little louder in surprise when she opened her hand and revealed the Moonstone necklace Bennie had been holding since Aila gave it to her. "What is it?" Bennie asked him as he gently lifted it from her hand.

"This is precious, Shadow," Perce said, "This was the last thing her husband gave her before he died."

"What?" Bennie jolted out of the strange peace she had been in. "What the hell is she giving it to me for!?!? I can't accept that from her!"

"Shadow, don't say the "h" word, and don't try giving it back, either," Perce said gently, stroking her hair to settle her down again. "She obviously sees something in you, something special, and she wanted you to have it. You'll probably need it too. Fairies have a way of knowing those things. A strong sense of Perception, in case you hadn't noticed."

"Something special in me," Bennie said bitterly, "What could she possibly see in a blind fifteen-year-old?"

"The same thing I do, Bennie," Perce said as he clasped the necklace on for her. Bennie pulled her hair up off her neck so the chain could slide into place. Bennie just blinked at him, hardly able to discern his shape at the moment.

"And what's that?" She asked him.

Perce was smiling at her, but it was sad.

"Hope, Bennie," he said to her. "I see hope, for the future."

Chapter Eight, Pictures

Bennie didn't remember falling asleep. She had almost forgotten what waking up in her own bed was like, with the natural insomnia that developed after acquiring of her powers. Even when her vision was basically gone, she could feel the blissfulness that only the mid-morning sunlight could create, pouring golden and bright into the room. It was slightly tainted with the late July heat, the one thing about living in South Texas that drove her mad. She had never lived anywhere else, and would probably never choose to leave on a whim, but she would have given anything for a thunder storm that day as she got ready for soccer practice. It hadn't rained since the day she became a Guardian, and the parched, yellow grass had taken up its bristly, burry feel under her hands and elbows again as she manned the goal net.

The sense enhancing potion she had taken that morning was doing more harm than help with the way it increased the heat of the sun on her bare arms, and her mind kept wandering to the shade of the live oaks she knew were on the other side of the fence.

Maybe Aila has another type that'll help me with heat tolerance.

"HEADS UP, BENNIE!" Bennie barely had time to get her mind back on the game before seizing a soccer ball that nearly passed her into the goal.

Focus! Bennie berated herself as she heard Julia Hernandez, the owner of the voice that had called her, mutter something teasingly in Spanish before placing up for the serve. Bennie couldn't help but grin. Julia was one of Bennie's oldest friendly soccer rivals and loved to pretend she was insulting Bennie in Spanish when she wasn't paying attention. Bennie was taking German instead, to be different, so she didn't know what Julia had really said.

It was something about "Santa Anna"-so I don't know how she can relate me to the Alamo...

Bennie suddenly felt so dizzy and hot, and before she knew it she had bolted from the goal post towards a secluded end of the field to be sick. Her limbs started shaking and she suddenly realized she had long since stopped sweating, and started drying up in the sun. How did she get so dehydrated so fast?

It's the heat, I can't handle it with these potions making me more sensitive to it, Bennie thought as several hands patted her on the back and handed her a bottle of water. *But I can't play without them, I'm dependent on them to alert me to my surroundings! How am I supposed to play soccer if I can't be outside for even half an hour?*

These thoughts pounded in her throbbing head as she relaxed under a ceiling fan in her living room (the rooms upstairs got really warm even with fans and air conditioning) while her younger cousin Timmy tried to cheer her up with his newest sketches, which was only making things worse since the heat stroke had left her heightened senses exhausted and useless even with the enhancers still in her system.

"See," Timmy said, unaware of his Bennie's predicament, "I'm going into plain pencil now, but the page looks all dirty because I smudge so badly. Last year Mrs. Clint at school said it's because I'm left handed and I should start on the right side of the page, but I can't help starting in the middle."

"Mmmm, good point," Bennie said, praying silently that Timmy wouldn't require specific observations from her at this point in time.

"Do you think this one looks a bit phony, though?" He stuck a blur in front of her. Bennie sighed, just her luck.

"Umm…" Bennie said, struggling to find something, *anything,* to say, finally giving into a partial truth. "I really can't tell, maybe when I'm not so out of focus. Sorry Timmy."

"Tim," Timmy corrected her. Bennie had forgotten he was going into the seventh grade now, and had dropped the two extra letters on his name upon entering middle school.

"Sorry." Bennie said, pulling a face. She hoped she didn't sound uninterested, even though she couldn't go on about pictures she couldn't see. She didn't want to be alone right now so it would probably be a good idea to keep Timmy talking.

"Tim," she said, remembering to shorten his name this time, "How can you tell what in a picture isn't right? When I took art for the credit last year, I could never figure out why my characters looked so fake. Some guy named Chen said it was the emotion, like, there wasn't any behind them when I created them."

"Yeah, you do better if you are feeling something for the picture, I think," Timmy said, and Bennie detected a hint of a "professional" tone in his voice. She suppressed a smile. "With me," he said, the tone definitely there this time, "I get the picture in my head and I can't get it to go away and leave me alone until I at least try to get it out. Those are the best ones, and they leave me with a much clearer head…"

Bennie didn't quite hear what he said next, her thoughts were jumbled again. Taking the picture out of the mind and onto the paper? Bennie wondered if that would take care of the image burned into the darkness on her eyes.

If only she could draw...

Chapter Nine, Tricks and Progress

Bennie had struggled all day on a piece of paper to try what her cousin had said, but every time she truly thought of what *it* had looked like she found herself shrinking away from the paper. She would begin to be able to see the paper and once she saw what was on it she couldn't get an actual picture all the way down before panic set in and the blackness covered her eyes again.

She felt tears coming on again. She had to get a grip on herself soon. She couldn't fool everyone forever, especially not her paranoid mother.

She'd kill Perce-as if it were his fault I was stupid. No, she'd kill him and then kill me, with a pair of rabid turtles eating me from the fingers and toes in.

"Bennie!" *Speaking of the devil.*

Bennie quickly jumped into bed, shoving her drawings under the pillow. She pulled a quilt around her and tangled herself in it a bit before she closed her eyes and evened her breathing.

There was a light thudding on the stairs. Bennie's door opened quietly. She didn't open her eyes. The door closed.

Bennie remained still for a while to make sure her mom didn't come up again. When she heard the car start she got up and looked out the window, despite the futility.

She felt the warm reflection of the sun on the car's roof move across her face. The whirr of the car's engine moved away down the road. Bennie was alone.

Bennie got up and tried the drawings again. No luck.

She went downstairs and threw herself on the couch. She put on the TV for a while but nothing good was on. Channel after channel of commercials. She sighed.

I would do my summer reading-if I could see the print on the pages, but I'm not focused like that yet.

Bennie pushed herself up off the couch and stormed out the front door. At least she knew the walk to school well enough to find her way to the source of the problem. All the running up there each night had to have some merit, night vision or no.

Bennie stopped when she reached the intersection where she had lost her eyesight.

Think. It was here. Don't push it away, remember...

The sun was too bright. She could feel it. It was so hot.

The sun's supposed to help me. Why do these sense enhancers drive me so crazy?

Bennie gave up and turned for home.

"What's up, Ben-jay?" someone said. Bennie jumped.

There was a car next to her that she hadn't noticed had stopped.

"Sean?" Bennie said.

"What're you doing out here?" Sean said.

"Thinking," Bennie said. She didn't want to get into it. She was beginning to feel hot and shaky again.

"I was just heading home from Hollywood Video," Sean said. "I picked up a game if you want to come hang out."

Bennie perked up. She didn't want to be alone but she was reluctant to go near her friends in case they noticed the fact she wouldn't look straight at them.

"Sounds like fun, but I'm no good with video games, especially not now," she said.

"Well we'll save the gaming for another time then," Sean said. "We've got plenty of movies, and we'll prank call Gemini!"

"I'm sure she'd like that," Bennie rolled her eyes. Sean laughed.

"Okay so our phones won't reach her area code or anything but we can always prank Perce's cell."

"Actually I wouldn't mind seeing him again-I mean-agh!" Bennie slapped her hand to her forehead. "This is pathetic."

"Here, get in and I'll take you to my place and we'll see if he can come over for a bit."

Sean got Bennie a soda while she called Perce to see if he minded stopping by.

"If you can hang on two more hours I'll come over." He said. "I'm just finishing up work."

"Work?" Bennie said. Somehow she had thought Perce's only job was training her and her friends. "What do you do?"

"I teach flying lessons." Perce's smile was evident even over the phone.

"I'd better stay on the ground then!" Bennie grinned. "What are you really doing, Perce?"

"I'm working with some pals on a project for the Guardians. I can't really talk about it, since it's all important and all that."

"Whatever you say, Perce," Bennie teased, but honestly she believed him. "See you when you get here-I mean-oh never mind."

"Yeah, I'll be there around 5-ish. Yo!" Perce hung up.

"So what are we going to do for two hours?" Bennie said to Sean. "Perce is at work but he's coming."

"Well there's always movies," Sean said. "Like the *Saw* movies?"

"Sick," Bennie said. "Put on *Dumbo* or something."

"*Dumbo* isn't politically correct," Sean said seriously. "How about some swashbuckling? *Muppet Treasure Island? Pirates of the Caribbean?*"

"Muppets!" Bennie bounced on the futon Sean had set up in his room. It was one of her favorite movies because Miss Piggy used her name-Benjamina-for her character. Soon they were rolling on the floor at the goofy pirates and even dopier crew of the treasure ship and Bennie forgot about the fact she was merely watching the movie out of memory.

Perce was almost an hour earlier than he had previously anticipated, and he and Bennie set to work on her blind-can-see act while Sean played the game he had picked up at the movie store.

"The drawing isn't working for you?" Perce said when Bennie told him about the idea she had gotten from her cousin Tim.

"No, I just sink back in again." Bennie said. "My only sign of progress is that I get a little further every time I do it."

"Well that's something," Perce said. "Going on location didn't help?"

"No, the sense enhancers make the sun a little too hot for me to focus. Trying to play soccer is going to be living hell-er-heck."

"Thanks for the correction," Perce was grinning again. "Living hellerheck."

Bennie laughed out loud.

"So!" Perce spoke again. "It's something to do with reliving what you saw. You need to be able to come to terms with it, which we've established, and you're trying, but we need to find the way to get it out of your system quickly before it takes over again. I'm thinking the fire."

"What about it?" Bennie said.

"You defended yourself with a fireball, right?" Bennie nodded. "Well, maybe fire can defend you again. We'll try some candle experiments tonight or something. Try going back and forth between fire and drawing."

Perce stood up.

"But I think we should get you home for now so you can rest a bit before practice."

"Home?" Bennie's heart stopped. Her mom would have to be home by now. It had been nearly three hours since she left.

"Uh-oh," Perce said, his tone serious as he read the expression that was obviously written all over her face. "You didn't let you mom know where you were did you? I know her well enough to know she'll freak out."

"I'm so grounded!" Bennie jumped up and made to run for the door, but she couldn't remember where it was and she couldn't locate it.

"I'll fly you home real quick," Perce said, and before Bennie could protest he propelled them out the window and across four miles.

"Perce be sure to land somewhere away from the house so I can run in without Mom seeing you!" Bennie said. That was trouble she could do without.

Perce dropped her off at the end of her street and Bennie bolted down the road to her house. She threw open the door and came in at full speed, crashing into her mom.

"I got you this for a reason you know!" Bennie felt her mom waving something in her face. A cell phone.

"I'm sorry!" Bennie said. "I just went out for a walk and some of my friends from soccer practice were-"

"I don't care, Benjamina!" Bonnie thundered. "I was only going to be gone for an hour, you should have realized that I'd come home and have a heart attack when I couldn't reach you!"

"I didn't *know* you were only going to be gone an hour!" Bennie shouted back.

"I left you a note!"

"Where!?!"

"Where I always leave notes! On the kitchen table!"

"I didn't see it! Okay? I just didn't see it!"

"Well have you gone *blind* or something?!?!"

Bennie stopped at that, horrified, before she realized her mom was just using an expression. Bennie huffed angrily.

"*Yes*, mom. I came across a monster the other night and he gave me the Oho and I'm so blind I can't even stop bumping into walls."

Bennie pushed past her mom and headed to her room.

"You don't go *anywhere* without telling me first from now on, you hear me?" Bonnie shouted after Bennie as she thudded up the stairs.

"As if!" Bennie muttered under her breath. Why could she never have a normal conversation with her mom? They could start one but would be mad at each other in five minutes because one or both of them would say something stupid.

Bennie's ill mood lasted into the night as she snuck out to practice after her mom was asleep. Perce was surprised to see her.

"I thought your mom would have surveillance cameras installed by now so you wouldn't be able to move a muscle all night without giving yourself away as a Guardian.

"The lump of blankets in the bed trick seems to work well enough," Bennie said, her irritation overly evident in her voice. Perce was quiet.

"I have something for you," Perce said after Bennie slumped down on a bench. "You mentioned the sun was too strong for you so Aila gave me this for you to take with your sense enhancers." He pressed a cold bottle of liquid into her hand. "It'll help keep you cooler without killing the effects of the enhancers."

"Thanks Perce," Bennie said. "But I don't know that they'll do me any good anyway. I'm still not good at getting my bearings just with my own personal radar system."

Perce clapped her on the shoulder. "That's why I thought we'd move our training to a different place, where the sun shines when we need it to. I'm going to get you to be 100% with these enhancers starting tomorrow, since tonight we're working with fire."

"How do you plan to get me to a sunny spot that can make my senses better?" Bennie said doubtfully.

"Easy!" Perce claimed. "Pelanca plus Soccer = blind yet fully functional!"

Chapter Ten, Soccer in a Midnight Sun

Bennie opened the window to let out the smoky smell she kept leaving in her room after every bout she had with the fire technique she was unsuccessfully using to get over "it." The fire just couldn't keep getting so big before she set something on fire, yet the small fire wasn't helping her at all since it felt like play acting in comparison to what she had reacted with that night almost a week earlier.

Her alarm went off. It was time for daily soccer practice, part two, with Perce. Bennie left the blankets bunched in the bed again and waited by the window for her lift.

Sean had begun carrying her–in full gargoyle form–from her window every night and taking her to class so she could avoid trouble from her mom–who now slept with the bedroom door open-and so he could get her straight to that place called Pelanca for practice. Perce had found an indoor field or something where he could make it hot and bright as day even when everything was dark or at a different time of day (Since Pelanca's time apparently ran so unevenly with Earth's) so he could have Bennie play soccer again and again until she could feel the field and team as well as she ever could see them. It was definitely helping her cover up on the real soccer field during the day time.

Bennie would have loved to cover up so well with her friends or at home. Both her friends and her mom were beginning to notice that her eyes always seemed dilated whenever she would actually look at them, and people were getting on her case for not finishing up her summer reading.

I'd just get someone who knows my problem to read to me but that would be cruel to them and I have to find some solution for during the school year-

Perce blew a whistle. The "team" he had conjured up or whatever he did to create two full soccer teams began moving. They were so like to her real team mates that she no longer needed them to shout for her to know who was who. She could tell simply by listening to the way they breathed which person was closest and who they were. Along with that, the heat bothered her less and less each day as the extra potion took effect.

But Bennie wasn't "100%" yet. She was now able to locate the ball on the field but she couldn't always keep tabs on it, or all the players, friend and foe, and her range of observation was still very limited. Today her problem was the ball coming to her by surprise right near the beginning of the game, and the tall, strong-kicking nameless opponent who kept coming up at an angle and stealing it before Bennie knew what had happened.

"Try not to focus so much on *every* team mate of yours once you have the ball, Bennie," Perce said. "You need to keep a radius of awareness around you so you can tell when someone's coming up."

"I feel like I'm learning self-defense, not soccer." Bennie groaned as she got up off the floor from where she'd fallen when her foot hit empty space instead of the ball.

"Well it's the same basic principle," Perce said. "You could fight in a battle with what you're learning simply to play a game right now-once you get it down right."

"Oh wow, somehow I've landed myself in the Army." Bennie joked.

"Army Reserve," Perce joked back, but his voice seemed oddly hollow. "We won't have you fighting any battles unless we have no choice."

Bennie was quiet after that. Perce had mentioned turbulence in the Guardians' world thanks to that Dark King, Reyortsed. She hadn't bargained on fighting any war, but she realized now her training wasn't just to keep her from setting the house on fire or electrocuting everyone, including herself, in a swimming pool.

I got these powers for a reason, not just randomly.

Bennie took to the field again, focusing on Perce's advice even more than she already had been. She drowned out the cheerleading antics Sean was making and trying to get Gemini into ("She'll need all the extra distractions we can give her for the real games, Gem!"). She barely heard the whistle that started the players moving.

Whoosh. The ball was coming. It was hers.

Bennie ran. She was supposed to make the goal…There was Sarah on her right, open for a pass…The goalie was at the far left of the net…she'd expect a right kick at the top…Bennie aimed for a top left…the goalie wouldn't be able to stop herself in time if she acted like she had been…

There was someone coming up behind her light-footed…

Bennie passed to Sarah just before the tall opponent got in her way. Sarah kicked the ball into the net so quickly that the goalie didn't even have time to register the change between players.

HAH! GOAL! Even if I didn't exactly score it myself…

"Good Bennie!" Perce shouted as the simulated game stopped. "You made the goal; the indirect approach was the trick. I think that's enough for tonight."

Bennie panted. She was out of breath after all the running. She felt for Perce's direction so she could face him.

"More tomorrow?" She said. She felt ready to take on anything right now after finally making the goal.

"Actually I thought I'd work with Sean a bit more tomorrow since his werewolf transformation is giving him so much grief. It'd give you time to work with the fire technique."

Bennie suddenly didn't feel like she could take on anything. Every time she had tried in the past week to fully visualize what she saw she had gotten a little farther, but she kept panicking and going dark in her eyes again. It was maddening.

"We're getting there Bennie," Perce said as they walked off the field to join Sean and Gemini, who had a new music piece ready for Perce to listen to. "Just keep trying."

Trying to see something I don't want to see, Bennie thought. *That seriously can't be good for me.*

Perce took Bennie home himself instead of letting Sean do it. Bennie found Perce's flying to be a little too fast for her liking, but she didn't want to hurt his feelings by saying no, even though she was sure he wouldn't mind, and probably already knew she liked the slower ride. He did keep the pace down a bit tonight, which was nice.

Perce landed Bennie inside her window after opening it with a charm from twenty feet up and hovered outside for a moment afterward.

"Bennie," he said when he saw the lump of blankets Bennie had left bundled under the covers on her bed. "Have you tried talking to your mom at all about being a Guardian?"

Bennie paused quietly, shaking her head guiltily.

"She wouldn't listen anyway," Bennie muttered. "She didn't want me seeing you, remember?"

"Bennie, this isn't just some rebellious midnight partying you're sneaking out for," Perce said. "This is very important and involves her as much as you or me. You can't keep lying to her."

"I'm not lying!" Bennie hissed. "I'm not saying anything at all. How is that lying? Ignorance is bliss isn't it?"

"Perhaps, but not for the likes of your mom," Perce said. "And sometimes silence is worse than the biggest lie. Good night Bennie."

Perce didn't fly away, he merely "dissolved" like he did that first night so many weeks ago, but Bennie thought about what he said.

How could mom knowing and being up all night fretting about me be better than letting her check on a lump of blankets so she can sleep peacefully?

Bennie couldn't sleep, and she couldn't get peace of mind either.

Maybe her mom didn't appreciate it, but Bennie would love to not have so many things to worry about.

Chapter Eleven, Sights of Darkness

Bennie's frustration lingered some as she crouched on the lumpy roots of a tree growing in the school courtyard while Perce and Gemini both struggled with Sean, whose last werewolf transformation had left him with a number of leftover wolf teeth that refused to be removed with a magic charm or otherwise.

"I think we may need Aila to work with these," Perce was saying as he tried to rot the teeth out while Gemini attempted to settle a very unsettled Sean down. The teeth weren't the only thing left over from his transformation. His relaxed attitude hadn't come through again yet.

"Yuhl wroth eh horng tiff!" Sean said around his new fangs.

"What?" Gemini said. Perce grinned.

"I think he's worried we'll get the wrong teeth," Perce said, amused. Gemini rolled her icy grey eyes at him.

"Really, how could we miss *those?*"

*The Teeth. How could I miss the huge, rotting bloody teeth, especially when they were still white…*Bennie felt every hair on her body rise.

"Sean, why don't you try transforming *back* into the werewolf again and maybe they will go away when you re-transform into a human?" Perce suggested. Sean started convulsing as he tried to morph again.

*It was like that. The body looked canine at first, but then it was nearly human...*Bennie shut her eyes tight, her hands growing hotter than ever. Adrenaline pulsing, she was back at the intersection...

"Well then, Perce, shouldn't we move away from him a bit in case he spasms again and claws one of us?"

*Not claws, talons...on the feet...the hands were- webbed or something...*Bennie felt the flames running through her veins.

Sean was groaning...it wasn't a human sound.

Nor was his voice...

"Yeah, I don't want another allergy attack with the fur..."

Was it really fur? The wings had scales, where they weren't rotting away...

"Aww look, Perce! Sean's giving us the puppy eyes!"

The eyes...oh, my god...he'll make me one too. I can see it in his eyes. "NO!"

Bennie screamed. The fire shot from her hand, blasting against the brick wall of the cafeteria, melting the glass on the doors. Her eyes snapped open and she turned to the horrific image in her mind, breathing raggedly, but a grin was coming. She could see *it* now, the horrible demon, with the fires of hell flickering behind his runny eyes, clear windows into his nonexistent soul.

"Gregk, you horror! You will not cripple me and you most certainly–"

More flames blasted into the wall

"CAN'T. HAVE. ME!"

The flames were roaring.

"I won't be afraid of you anymore!"

Bennie blasted the side of the cafeteria again and again, unblinkingly staring at Gregk the demon, his image frozen in that moment where she had last seen the world through her real eyes. Her hand shot lightning once, twice, and then she lay panting, the image more vivid than ever, but not gone.

The moonstone pendant suddenly felt heavy, and Bennie turned her eyes upward toward the moon, shining, full now.

Bennie panted, staring up at it, barely aware of the arms lifting her up.

"Bennie..." It was faint. Bennie blinked.

"Bennie!" Clearer now. Bennie's view of the moon was obscured by a shape...a face...familiar, yet oddly sharper than Bennie had seen since the—

Wait a minute. *Seen?*

Bennie's brain finally registered Perce's face. She was indeed *looking* at him.

"Hey..." Bennie said, a smile creeping on her lips. "I think I did it!"

It took Perce a minute to realize what Bennie was talking about, or even if *she* knew what she was talking about.

"You mean..."

"Perce, when was the last time you trimmed your beard? There's one hair right below your right ear that's at least an inch longer than the others." Bennie teased.

"Hey!" Perce laughed, helping Bennie to her feet, and hugging her. Bennie didn't think she'd felt this good before, not even when Perce had shown her how to feel the moonlight on the roof. It finally hit her that she finally had rid herself of something she should have just up and faced a long time ago. It wasn't so bad, was it?

She tried to wipe the tears away quickly but they kept coming until Sean produced a handkerchief, claiming he would frame it the day his "Lovely Gem" called for its help. Then he ducked a swat from said Gem.

"And while we were all hiding behind a force field Perce remembered to put up during your lovely artistic inspiration Ben-Jay," Sean said, "I did something of my own-look! No teeth! Well, none of the dog teeth are left. That's what I mean."

Bennie laughed and looked nervously at the wall of the cafeteria. She had been right, the image of Gregk she had still seen after blasting him from her mind was burned into the wall and doors in full detail, lacking only the death in the eyes, but she stared at it hard. He would not frighten her anymore. Only after regaining her sight did she realize how dreadful life without it had been, how life fearing his horrible features had been.

Perce slowly began repairing the damage to the wall, as if waiting for Bennie to say she needed to see it a bit longer, but Bennie didn't. Her mind had already moved from Gregk's image to the sudden vacancy beside her. She was cold now that Perce had moved away, like she did when her mother got off the couch when they were watching one of their favorite Sandra Bullock movies. She hated that feeling, it was like being abandoned.

But Perce was still right there. He hadn't run away, just gone to fix something.

"Bennie," Perce said, snapping her out of her brief zoning. "We're supposed to report to Aila right away if anything like this happened. Get your stuff together, you guys. We're going to Pelanca."

"Woo-hoo! I Looooveee Pelanca!" Sean said. "Really, all those super-chicks-"

"Of course he'd want to go for that!" Gemini sniffed. She seemed genuinely irritated at first but after she turned away from Sean she winked at Bennie. It was obviously an old tactic of Sean's to make her jealous.

"But none are as super or as beautiful as our lovely Gem!" Sean threw himself on his knee in front of the young goddess, who in turn flicked a fleck of some golden dust from her fingers into his face. He sneezed.

"None of that, you two!" Perce said with a distracted grin as Sean sneezed again. And again. "Gemini, get it off him." Perce opened what looked to be a compact mirror from the outside.

"Not yet!" Gemini said, "He can't flirt if he's sneezing."

"Ah, but he'll attract attention and sympathy from those super-chicks if they think he has allergies!" Bennie said, grinning. "And since I'll actually be able to *see* this Pelanca place I don't want to be stopping for all the doting they'll drop on him."

"True, but it would get him off me for a bit," Gemini said, but nonetheless she snapped her fingers and Sean promptly stopped sneezing.

"Gee, I like a girl with a home cure for cleaning out the sinuses," Sean said, blowing his nose.

"Well he won't be having any time for home remedies from anyone in Pelanca," Perce said, coming back into the conversation and closing the strange little compact mirror. "Guess who plans to catch us tonight while we're in town?"

"Who?" Bennie said before seeing the looks on Sean and Gemini's faces. Perce was grinning wickedly again.

"You're not serious!" Sean said. "It's been ages since he's had time to go out interacting with people! I haven't seen him since when I had passed the gargoyle-shifting!"

"Well, you'll get a better introduction this time since it's not an emergency, he just wants to meet Bennie and have a little talk with me on our way out." Perce said.

"Not to sound stupid, but *who* wants to meet me?" Bennie said, nervous at the amount of shock and awe generating from her comrades as they looked at her.

"Wow, Bennie, you must be really special if *he's* coming to meet you," Gemini said, staring at Bennie curiously, "We're talking about *Esla,* the Leader of the Guardians."

"What? He wants to meet me? What for?"

"Well," Perce said, shifting uncomfortably, "I think it's because your powers are so unique. Esla's power is adaptation, instant skill. Basically he touches a person and instantaneously gains a copy of their powers and abilities for a short while. He uses it to figure out ways to train people to the highest they can perform. No one's quite sure how far your powers can go yet, so he may want to find out for himself. He was the best training officer the Guardians ever saw. He became our Leader when Heimdall disappeared about a year ago. No one ever did know what happened to him. He vanished during a major skirmish with some of Reyortsed's followers that had not left with him but stayed to spy. Sean last met Esla during the fight after he finally hit his gargoyle-shifting during the panic and helped protect some civilians."

"Wow, you never told me this, Sean!" Bennie said.

"Yes, our own little hero," Gemini tweaked Sean's ear affectionately, and the ear turned pink enough for Bennie to see even in the dim light before it was dark enough for her to see plainly.

"It-it's not uncommon, you know." Sean said, but his ears only turned pinker.

"But anyway, enough time for stories later," Perce said, "We have to get going if we're going to make the appointment. Who's flying with who?"

It took Bennie a second to realize Perce was talking about getting to Pelanca. He always shot himself around like a rocket, which made Bennie sick when he flew her too.

"I'll take Bennie," Gemini quickly said, "I don't trust Sean to be still on the way down."

"Aww!" Sean protested, "But Perce speeds! I think we're going to crash every time we come to a corner he goes so fast! He's done it before you know!"

"Not since I was a rookie, and I only go fast because I can't fly if I don't!" Perce said. "Seriously, Sean, where's your enjoyment of thriller rides?"

"But, hold on!" Bennie said. "Sean, you can transform into that Gargoyle, you've flown me down there every day for over a week. Couldn't you fly yourself?"

"The nearest route to Pelanca is too narrow for that shape," Sean said pointing toward the far end of the school. "I take a different way when I take you.

"Now if we were practical we'd buy ourselves a personal transporter and avoid the whole mess, but Perce refuses to block up a room in his apartment for us to arrive in."

"Flying is more fun anyway," Perce said decisively. "If y'all want to fill up your living space with a hunk of junk like a transporter or to find a safe hiding place around all these normal and overly-curious people be my guest, but find a different place to put the receiving end from my apartment. But we've got to *move*. This is *Esla* we're talking about you guys, he'll be busy so we don't want to keep him waiting."

And with a bunch of good natured grumbling from Sean they hurried to the back field of the school and one by one slid down a storm drain at the far end of the passing sidewalk. Bennie didn't think they could fit through the narrow opening but the visible size was obviously some sort of forced perspective to make it inconspicuous to the casual eye. She slid through last without any trouble at all.

Once inside she found to her left a hole large enough for a human to walk in with ease: down, down, down. The drain continued off to her right into the sewers. Perce had already grabbed Sean and was rocketing off into the black abyss.

"Hold on," Gemini said, pulling Bennie against her like Perce had done on Bennie's first exit of Pelanca via the strange tunnel network.

And with that she darted into the hole.

Chapter Twelve, Pelanca

Bennie instantly noticed a difference in Gemini's flying compared to Perce's. Perce always whizzed around something like a supersonic bumble bee. Gemini still went fast, but smoothly and much slower, like a fast car. Bennie wasn't sure which way she liked more. She didn't get sick with Gemini like she did with Perce, but it wasn't as fun, like comparing the Superman roller coaster to the Scream at Fiesta Texas. The Scream just always fell short.

This particular tunnel had apparently been made as a one-way backstreet to the heart of the Guardian civilization because it had no intersections and went straight to the strange city that was God-knows-where. They got there remarkably fast considering the obvious distance. Perce was leaning up against the wall of the large cavern they had landed in when Gemini and Bennie arrived. Sean was bent over a trash can a few paces away, green in the face.

"I don't like flying with him," Sean said to Bennie as he gratefully took a water bottle from Perce, who looked sheepish at first, then set into teasing Gemini.

"It took you guys long enough, we've been here about—" Perce looked at his stopwatch. "—Forty-two seconds longer than you. Hah! My lucky number. You've slowed up a bit, Gem."

"I had a passenger, which is unusual for me," Gemini said passively and left whatever competition there was at that.

Bennie walked toward the sunlight coming out of the cave mouth. She couldn't imagine anywhere on earth they could be, especially since they surely had not crossed the international date line in two minutes.

"Welcome to Pelanca, Bennie!" Sean said just as Bennie looked out from the mouth of the cave.

Upon entering the city limits Bennie had to gasp. She had been to Pelanca before but she had never *seen* it. It took her breath away as she stared and stared, taking in as much as possible.

The city was made of thousands of different kinds of buildings. Some looked very old, others very new, but all looked well cared for. The mass of buildings stretched beyond sight, domes and spires, glass, steel and stone. The architecture ranged from familiar modern and Renaissance to foreign and unthinkable designs.

The sun was just rising, setting the city glittering and glowing, shining off the silvery lakes and streams Bennie saw about. Surrounding the city was nothing but green meadows on the yet unmarked hills that footed the tall, distant mountains, and trees with an occasional small farm of sorts raising animals and fruits and vegetables.

There were no cars, only odd, quiet pod-like vehicles that flew as well as drove and sailed on the water. There were dragons, some alone, others carrying one or more people. Some fairies flew themselves above the city, teaming with tiny people, far below. There was no city racket, only the quiet hum of life. There was no pollution.

It was beautiful.

"Man, I love to finally see someone else' first reaction to this city," Sean said. "We should get new classmates more often!"

Bennie blinked in surprise and laughed. "Was I really drooling that much?"

"Your jaw was on the floor!" Sean teased.

They set off down the slope into the city. Bennie wasn't so surprised by the city itself as she was by the fact that its subtle differences from a normal city like San Antonio seemed to have no affect of shock on anyone else.

"Perce, where is this Pelanca city?" Bennie said, "There's no way it can just be anywhere on earth. People wouldn't take too well to dragons and all that."

"Whoever said we were on Earth, Bennie?" Sean spoke up before Perce could.

"What?" Bennie said.

"We're not in our world, Bennie," Perce said. "Pelanca's not just a city."

"Not in our world...there's more than one then?" Bennie said.

"Of course!" Sean laughed. "My friends aren't far off when they say there is alien life out there somewhere. They just don't know I know the aliens, like Gemini!"

"Oh, I forgot about that," Bennie grinned sheepishly, while Gemini made a face behind Sean's back.

"There are thousands of worlds," Perce said, but before he could explain further they came to what seemed to be the heart of the city: A huge dome of a building surrounded entirely by water and open greens. The one bridge that led to the building was decorated with an elaborate and ancient set of gates. They were made of a silvery green swirled metal very much like the water in the "moat" the building sat within.

Bennie studied the gates with interest as the group drew closer. They were wrought with elegant designs and runes that glinted in the sun. But Bennie was more interested in the strange creatures guarding the gates from their perches on either side. They were some strange sort of birds, powerful gold-feathered hawks with sharp talons and clever keen eyes. They merely glanced at the newcomers before eyeing their surroundings again.

"Lewelines," Gemini said, "They come from the Elven world."

"Lay-vel-leens," Bennie said, "The Elven world? So there are thousands of these planets?"

"Well, technically yes, but some worlds are in the same place as others, on different realms of reality, but the worlds overlap where this world, Pelanca is, somehow. The underground tunnels are actually magical roads that lead to this place. All the worlds connect here so you can pass from one end of the universe to the other in mere minutes instead of millennia.

"The Lewelines are just an example of the mingling this place is. The buildings are another. Every culture leaves something here and it makes this city unique."

"So do those gates come from the Elves too? I saw the runes."

"The gates come from the same world, yes, but it's not Elfin. It is fairy craft. The fairies also live there, but their language is complicated to speak as it involves the use of their wings as well as their voice, so the runes are actually the Dwarves' magic charms of protection. The gates are made from the fairy River Metal. Supposedly it's one of the strongest substances in the known universe."

"So the Fairies and Elves and Dwarves all put something into those gates that protect this place..." Bennie said.

"Exactly," Sean said. "It's the Guardian Capital, in a way, our stronghold. And the humans came up with the general design of the building."

"So every race gave something to this one building?" Bennie said, impressed.

"There are a lot more races and worlds than just those," Perce said, "But yes, most of them have put something into this building, or the city itself."

Bennie thought hard about this new knowledge as they walked past the gates and around the enormous dome. They made their way through a wide, green and well-manicured field filled with men and women practicing fighting techniques with basic weapons as well as their powers. Bennie saw one blonde girl pull a move that looked like a figure-skater spin and split apart into little white-hot balls of fire to melt a set of Chinese Tai Chi Wind and Fire Wheels a training coach had thrown at her. The coach then melded them back to normal with a single blow from his lips. Further down, over a net, a series of young men were hurling themselves off a scaffold into the open air above the net, sprouting wings or morphing completely into some sort of bird or other winged creature, and wielding mock weapons as they practiced flying maneuvers. Their coach swooped on dark grey wings around each individual, parrying their blows and barking instructions as he inevitably brought them all down, panting, onto the net.

"Hey Marek!" Perce called to the coach, "Don't let them wear you out!"

"Perce! Good to see you've not broken your neck yet!" The coach called without breaking concentration on fighting the young elf that simply walked on the air like it was solid ground. "And you're supposed to call me Saxton around the newbies! I made a bet they'd never guess my real name until they beat me in training and now I've lost!"

Perce laughed.

"Alright, Mr. 'I go by my night name for money!' I'll keep it in mind!"

The coach–Marek or Saxton or whatever he chose to be called– waved with one hand before sending the elf sailing into the net with an "umph!"

"Old friend," Perce said to Bennie.

Perce took Bennie to see Aila while Gemini and Sean stayed outside to watch the people training across the road.

Bennie was happy to see–and really see– the wizened yet not aged face of her fairy friend. Aila also seemed pleased that Bennie had managed to master the crippling fear that had bound her. But when she peered deep into Bennie's eyes, she frowned slightly.

"There's still a shadow of the fear there, I'm afraid," she said. "Not unusual, I'd expect-many people come through trauma with a lingering scar. But I fear it may cause trouble if ever you face that kind of terror again. You'll have to learn to keep it from overcoming you or you'll be left helpless and blind again."

"We'll work with it," Perce said, "Bennie's a tough cookie like her dad. She can handle it."

Bennie blinked. She knew Perce knew her dad, but he never said anything about him.

There was a roar of "Ooooh!" from outside. Apparently some sort of friendly battle of wits was taking place on the battle field.

"I'm going to go check it out," Perce said curiously, and left Bennie and Aila alone in the room. Aila pottered around a bit, thinking out loud to herself while making notes about Bennie's condition on a clipboard.

"Aila, I-I never got to thank you properly for the necklace," Bennie said awkwardly. "Perce told me what it meant, and I really don't know if I could accept it now."

Aila smiled. Her wings fluttered slightly and she clicked her ballpoint pen shut.

"A true treasure is one shared, not locked away, Bennie," She said.

"But it's more than just a necklace or something, it's invaluable," Bennie tried again.

"Bennie, I *want* you to have it," Aila said. "You need it more than I do! It's like giving your younger sibling your lucky bear so they can sleep at night since you've outgrown the monsters in the closet. Yes, it is a treasure, but it can only make me happy if I know it's not going to be locked up in my treasure box to never see life and love again."

Bennie put her hand over the moonstone pendant she never took off. "I don't know how to show you how much I appreciate it." She finally said.

Aila fluttered up to the bed Bennie sat on and smoothed the chain of the necklace carefully.

"Just take care of it and of yourself, and that will be enough," She said.

Chapter Thirteen, Esla

Bennie joined Perce outside, keeping a protective hand over the pendant Aila had given her. She was shocked to find Gemini standing on the practicing grounds, radiating glory in her full goddess form. She was rigid, facing a fierce glare at another goddess across the field. Bennie thought they were having a standoff at first, but Perce was smart enough to inform her right away what was really going on before she panicked.

"Don't worry, Gemini's just doing a coach a favor. He needed another goddess to help with his student's telekinetic training," he told Bennie. "Gemini's good at keeping one position, even with magical force, so she volunteered. You never know when you'll be needed around here."

"What was the ooohhing about?" Bennie asked.

"Oh, Sean was just being a flirt again, and Gemini's good with comebacks." Perce grinned wickedly as he watched Gemini began to lift off the ground, and pushed herself back down again against the will of the other goddess.

"What did she say?" Bennie asked.

"Nothing." Perce shrugged her off.

"Tell me!"

"Why?"

"Because I'd like to know."

"Well then, do you know the Elfish myth about the Dog and the Lemur?"

"No…" Bennie looked at him, confused.

"Well then, it wouldn't make any sense to you."

"Well, first tell me the myth, *then* tell me the joke!"

"Can't. Don't know the myth."

"Well then how did you get the joke?!?!?!"

"I'm *Perseus!* I get every joke!"

Bennie just stared at Perce in exasperation.

"You like to annoy me don't you?"

"Yup."

Just then, Gemini sunk about three feet into the ground, which – Bennie noted – was solid and compact. Bennie realized the other student must have relinquished her telekinetic hold on Gemini and the sheer force Gemini had been using to hold herself down was suddenly unnecessary.

Everyone laughed and cheered as Gemini pulled herself out of the dirt and dusted herself off, bowing courteously and receiving more laughs. Her opponent massaged her temples and shook her head, smiling in amazement.

"Wow, Gem!" Sean said from Bennie's right somewhere in the crowd. "You could get a paying job working with that group!"

"Sorry, you're still the Lemur," Gemini said to him, and everyone roared with laughter again before departing.

Bennie just stared blankly.

"*Are* there really lemurs in the Elf world?" Bennie asked.

"No," Gemini said, "I'll explain the Dog and Lemur myth someday when we've got plenty of sitting time."

"You promise?"

Perce nodded. "Either her or me. But as much as I hate to break up the party, there's a certain someone waiting for us at Headquarters." Perce led them along the field again towards the Dome.

Immediately upon entering the Dome Bennie was struck with the same feeling that stepping into the State Capitol had given her when she went on the field trip to Austin in the seventh grade. Only this time the feeling was magnified about six times by the sheer size of the building she was in.

A vast interior of pale green polished marble was her first glimpse of its glory and the sheer height of the ceiling made even the dizzying rotunda of the Capitol seem obsolete.

Bennie followed Perce to the left through a set of elaborately carved doors that appeared to be plated in bronze. *Fancy.* She thought to herself.

They entered another marble corridor that was much narrower than the main lobby but with many more doors. Some of the doors were open, and Bennie saw that one of them was a library of sorts. Other rooms held long tables and computers and filing cabinets. A classic building of archives and diplomacy, it would seem, but nonetheless curiously interesting. Bennie thought her interest in the contents of the building probably had something to do with the fact it contained more information about the other worlds and the Guardians than she could ever hope to learn.

Perce led her, Sean, and Gemini up a long, wide staircase to the second floor, then up another to the third. Despite the modern computer technology Bennie had seen on the first floor, the Headquarters of the Guardians apparently lacked the luxury of elevators.

Probably because people with magic are prone to accidents, and enclosed spaces are a bad idea, Bennie thought with a smile, remembering Gemini sinking four feet into the solid earth without breaking her legs. Going straight through the floor of an elevator could cause problems, whether Gemini could fly or not.

"Here we are," Perce said as they approached a door with two Guards on either side. Neither had any obvious weapons, but considering this strange world Bennie had stepped into, she doubted they needed guns or other obvious tools of violence. The black suits and sunglasses made Bennie think of the CIA, and she felt like she was about to meet the President – only that he'd have Elfin features like the guards.

Bennie expected a lot more show of security than she got. The guards simply looked at them and seemed to know right away they were unarmed and had good intentions. Then the large bronze doors behind them opened, and the foursome hurried inside.

"Perce," Bennie had to ask, "Why exactly are they letting us in so easily?"

"They're not," Perce said, smiling at her, "When we crossed the threshold of this room, our powers were neutralized, and their glasses are equipped with the latest weapon detection systems, among other things. You can't beat combined Human, Elf and Fairy technology, you know. Only Esla can turn our powers back on as long as we're in this room."

"Did someone call my name?" A deep, soft but stern voice said. Its owner stepped out from behind a partition that separated the lounge-like area they had entered from a more office-like area. Bennie noticed an open door in the far corner behind a large desk. She could see through the open door that shadows were moving on the wall within.

But Bennie's attention was quickly drawn to Esla, who was unlike anyone she had seen before, though she couldn't place what it was about him that struck her so.

He was a tall, Elven man with an angled face devoid of wrinkles. His dark grey eyes glittered and his silver hair was pulled back and hung long over his shoulders. He wore a long robe of an off-white color stitched in silver, and despite his dignified, foreboding demeanor, Bennie felt this was a leader who could be loved, trusted, and would do so in return.

That feeling only grew stronger as a small elf girl with silvery-gold hair and deep blue eyes came scampering through the door behind the desk, ran up behind him, and tugged at his robe. He picked her up, bouncing her on his arm as he spoke to Perce, and Bennie liked him instantly.

"Perseus, I'm glad you came," He said, shaking Perce's hand. "I'm being called back to Dwendol in three days, and I don't know when we'll get this chance again."

"It's good to see you again," Perce smiled warmly before taking on seriousness again. "Are there still signs of a possible rend around Dwendol, then?"

"We're doing our best to prevent it," Esla said, and turned his attention to Sean.

"Hadrian, you're doing well? You've grown more than Aurelia, if that's possible," The little Elf girl giggled as he tweaked her nose. Bennie realized she was Aurelia.

"No, I'd say our little Goldilocks here has beaten me by quite a bit," Sean said, nodding to Aurelia, who smiled and hid her face in her father's robe.

"And Gemini, how you are holding out against these two rascals?" Esla smiled almost Perce-like, but it seemed different, like he couldn't quite get the many years of a long life away from his eyes entirely. It made Bennie sad, in a way, to see someone who couldn't forget enough to remember how to smile. It occurred to her then that Elves were immortal.

"Oh, I think I'm holding out well against the insanity I'm surrounded by," Gemini said, throwing on a mock serious face. "It's Bennie I'm worried about. She might turn into another one and then I'll be stuck!"

It didn't take long for her to break into a bright smile and admit she would be bored to tears without the bunch of them.

Then Esla turned his gaze onto Bennie. She almost shivered, though his gaze wasn't cruel. Rather, he seemed almost as awed by her as she did him. Bennie also realized Aurelia had lifted her face out again, and was staring at her with her extremely blue eyes wide.

"And Bennie, you must be Shadowchild," Esla said, taking her hand in his gently.

"It's an honor to meet you, sir," Bennie said, feeling stupid.

"No, no, the pleasure is mine," Esla smiled, "I understand you came into your powers a little over a month ago?"

"Five weeks," Bennie said.

"Well, if you all would like to come with me, we'll see what we can learn about just how much you can do," he said. "Oh, and this little wide-eyed-wonder is my daughter Aurelia," He bounced Aurelia again, and she blinked, and smiled. Bennie smiled back.

"Hello," she said, and Aurelia hid her face again.

"She's a bit shy," Esla said, making a face that could have made Bennie laugh. His eyebrows slanted straight up into a worry knot between his eyes and his lower lip came over the top one unevenly. It was an expression Bennie had seen on many parents' faces when they did not quite understand something about their child, and weren't sure whether they should be concerned or not. It seemed odd one of the most powerful leaders in the world…er…worlds, could be uncertain about something as simple as his little daughter's social skills.

"Most of them do start out shy," Bennie said. "Soon you'll be wishing she wasn't so friendly to everyone."

"Probably true!" Esla laughed, letting Aurelia slide down on to her own feet. She turned toward the group and smiled.

"*Tennai!*" she said, giving Bennie one last wide-eyed smile, and she scampered off back through the door in the far corner.

Bennie watched Aurelia's shadow on the wall beyond the door. Another shadow quietly joined it. Bennie assumed it was her mother.

"Well then," Esla said, "Shall we?"

The foursome followed Esla out through the doors, past the guards, and down the hall. They went to into another room that was devoid of any furniture, and the marble walls appeared to have some sort of protective covering on them.

"We don't want any accidents damaging the building," Esla said when he saw Bennie's curious look. "The dwarves are really good with diamond-proofing anything."

Sean seemed amused when Esla said that, and Esla winked at him. Bennie would have to ask what that was all about later.

As for the diamond-proofing, Bennie didn't even want to think about how expensive that would be in her world.

Esla was speaking again.

"So you blend into shadows and can see through the dark," he said, blacking out part of the room with a control panel on the wall, "You also control flame and electricity, ejecting it through your palms."

"That's right," Bennie said. Esla started walking towards the darkened area of the room. Much to Bennie's surprise, he began to dissolve before her eyes.

But then she realized he wasn't dissolving, he was *blending*, just like she did.

"Hey-wha-?" She started. Perce and the others laughed.

"That's his power, Bennie, remember?" Perce said. "When he touched your hand he acquired your abilities-only for about half an hour, but even so, it's long enough to help you figure out all your capabilities."

"Weird," Bennie said, remembering now. "Cool, but weird."

"Fascinating," Esla's voice came from within the shadows. "It's almost like your eyes don't need any more than starlight to see, or even less. As for the blending, your body just melds its colors, like a chameleon. I suggest you should wear darker clothes to help, since brighter ones can still stand out."

Bennie was thinking about creeping into the shadows herself and checking her skin out when Esla called on her.

"Bennie, would you mind pressing the green button on the control panel, please?"

Blinking, Bennie reached out and pressed it. She wasn't the only one who jumped a mile when the explosion of flames and lightning came straight for them. But the button she had pressed had activated some sort of force field because the flames rolled back before they touched them. The lightning was just absorbed into the field.

Bennie nearly panicked when the fire struck Esla but it left no mark on him, not even on his clothes.

The flames dwindled as Perce turned the lights back on, revealing an extremely impressed Esla. Perce was grinning at Sean, who had jumped in front of Gemini and pushed her against the wall when the fire came. He was currently receiving a vicious but amused look from his charge.

"Did you know you were fireproof?" Esla said to Bennie.

"I'm *what?*" Bennie asked.

"Apparently you didn't," Esla smiled. "It seems your natural defense against backfire-literally speaking- is to simply not burn. I assume that protection covers electric shock as well."

"So," Bennie was still trying to register this new information, "Not only can I walk through a burning building unharmed, I'll never get static shock again. What else am I going to find out about myself?"

"Who knows, but I've been doing this sort of thing for many years," Esla said. "After a while one begins to feel deeper into the traits of each power."

"Well, do you know what those powers will be, or what they'll do, like, to the fireproof skin I seem to have?"

"Only time will show us, I'm afraid," Esla said, looking at Perce. Then he changed the subject.

"Even though your skin is fireproof, I highly doubt anything in your wardrobe is. Perseus will take you to the shops downstairs to find the right clothes for the job."

"I don't have any money." Bennie said.

"You won't need it," Esla said reassuringly as they left the diamond-coated room and headed for Esla's office. "Everyone who works in this building is supported financially by the Guardian government, so they don't need to charge you for their products. We supply them, they supply you."

"Makes sense," Bennie said.

When they reached Esla's office, he turned to Bennie, lifting up his hand and shooting small darts of electricity to the ceiling.

"There's not much more for you to do other than practice such maneuvers you are already learning until your new powers show up. Let Perce know of any changes you notice, understood?"

Bennie nodded and looked at Perce. Though he was hiding it well, he seemed to have a lot on his mind. She noticed the tattoo on his finger again, the one that matched the mark on her shoulder. Something clicked.

The mark and the tattoo must be linked to my undeveloped power. Why aren't they just saying so?

Bennie was about to speak up about her observation when Esla spoke again.

"I must leave you now, but I have another new student coming in. Apparently she has a curious relationship with insects."

"Don't let her near me!" Sean said. "I'm allergic to half of them!"

And with that they headed down the stairs to the clothing shops.

* * *

"So, Bennie has the right to bear firearms?" Sean remarked, poking her on the shoulder as they left the shop with some fashionable yet practical clothes Gemini had helped Bennie pick.

"You two can't be trusted with things like clothes shopping!" Gemini had teased the men. Perce had been indignant.

"What, my lovely scruffiness isn't 'in' enough for girls these days?" he said, flipping back his overgrown, curly mess of hair in a both humorous and disturbing way.

"Actually, I think it's the beard, man." Sean had observed with a very serious expression.

"Oh, maybe I should shave!" Perce said.

"No, you'd look too weird without it," Bennie had wrinkled her nose at the thought as they had entered the shop. Now as they left she brushed Sean's poking finger away from her shoulder.

"I should hope I have my right to bear firearms, because they're the only arms I have!" She teased. "And the poking will make them fall off. Where would I be then?"

"But you like soccer-which is all feet," Sean said.

"Oh, I *roll* my eyes at thee!" Gemini said dramatically, but she was grinning too.

"Not to change the subject or anything," Sean said, "But are you alright, Perce? You look, I dunno...out of it."

"I'm good," Perce said, but Bennie could see the same thing that Sean was seeing. Perce was obviously distracted about something. But he just smiled at them and continued on.

"I'm a little tired I think. I don't sleep every night you know, and it's been about two months since I did," He said.

Bennie raised an eyebrow at Sean and Gemini. Gemini shrugged.

"I think I could use a little sleep myself tonight," Bennie said, trying to take the pressure off Perce. She trusted him to know what he was doing, and worrying him about the fact they were worrying was apparently the last thing he needed.

True to her word, Bennie did need sleep that night. When she finally dropped off she had the strange dream with the faces of the other Guardians again. But it was different this time.

Now there was a man, tall and slim but strong, with torrents of long black hair shadowing his face. Shadows Bennie couldn't penetrate. Then he turned and stared straight at her. His eyes, like his hair, were black, stark night against the twilight grey of the Guardians' eyes. It was all she could see of his face in the cloaking of his hair, but it was enough to make her back away into the arms of the Guardians. But she could not escape those eyes, haunting and beautiful, but *dangerous.*

The word rang in her head like a bell, and she woke with a start. But before she could comprehend what had happened she slipped back into her dreams. These were different, the simple dreams she normally had, and by morning, the black-eyed man was forgotten among them.

Chapter Fourteen, Rend

The next day Bennie didn't have soccer practice or training to ready herself for, so she settled on the couch for some summer assigned reading. She wanted to finish it as soon as possible so she could get the essay about the book's theme over with. It was just as well Bennie had begun to like writing more the year before because, thanks to her blindness, she was behind schedule on the summer work that had driven her nuts the year before.

She wasn't expecting the phone to ring, and she most certainly didn't expect it to be Gemini, saying Perce needed them to come train that night anyway.

When Bennie arrived that night, Sean and Gemini were already there, arguing with each other why Gemini didn't try a human high school for the fun of it. Perce was nowhere to be seen.

"*Funny,*" Bennie said loudly over the other two to get their attention. "Perce is never late."

"Yeah," Sean said, "Do y'all know what's on his mind? He was really kind of disquieted earlier."

"It probably has something to do with Dwendol," Gemini said to Sean, "The possible rend, you know?"

"Who-what?" Bennie said.

"Oh, sorry Bennie," Gemini said, "Rends...hmm where to start...well, the Dark Forces may be lurking about, but they're subdued to the point of being unable to take control of the passage between the worlds the Fairies created centuries ago."

"Whooaah, okay back up and tell me again, what passageway? Sorry." Bennie blushed.

"Yeah, good idea," Sean said, "Pelanca."

"Oh, Duh," Bennie grinned.

"So way back when, some old Fairy philosophers discovered this flat continuum in the universe, a plane of reality that overlapped all the other realities. It connects the various parts of the universe that could never be reached on linear distance, if this makes any sense at all."

"I think I get it," Bennie said.

"So they started watching the other worlds from there," Gemini said, "Eventually they began communications with other important people until almost all the worlds were united. Pelanca was the land they built on the overlapping plain and they opened channels-the underground tunnels we take-between the worlds to Pelanca. It's the central hub of known existence; everyone crosses through there. Mostly just the Guardians use it now though as most people in the worlds live ignorant of the other worlds or have little need to travel."

"Okay," Bennie said. "That's weird, but it makes sense. How did we get on this topic again?"

"Um," Gemini looked up as if to find the thought floating above her head.

"Rending," Sean grinned. "I have good backtracking skills."

"Oh that's right," Bennie said, "So what is 'rend?'"

"A rend happens when the enemy tries to break through into the other worlds or Pelanca without using the passages. We control Pelanca, so they can't get through that way. Rends are dangerous because they can and often do have negative effects on the worlds in question. I mean, you're simply ripping space and time open, and they can attract attention from normal people for that reason and for the skirmishes that follow to combat the intruders. Luckily they're also rare because making one is complicated-"

"-And the magic and manpower involved can, and has, cost many powerful magicians their lives." Gemini finished for Sean. "But there's a problem. There are more of them now than ever."

"You can thank Reyortsed and his wonderful ability to recruit more people to his side for that. He was also the reason for the attack on Pelanca I was in two years ago."

"He made a rend through *Pelanca?*" Bennie said, shocked.

"I know," Sean said. "He's not the first to attempt that particular stunt, but he is the first to actually come through with it, which is why he's such a threat."

"Whoever controls Pelanca controls traffic between the other worlds, and not to mention the worlds themselves," Gemini said. "But he's not attacking Pelanca now, he's attacking Dwendol, my home world." The worry on Gemini's face was unnerving to Bennie, who knew Gemini as the witty, smooth and slightly cynical member of the group.

"It could just be a decoy," Sean said, trying to put a hand on Gemini's shoulder. She brushed it away. "A distraction to drive us away from Pelanca."

"If that's supposed to make me feel better, it didn't," Gemini said. "Attacks on Dwendol or any world is a problem, but Pelanca is a disaster. So no decoys please."

"Not to lighten the mood or anything," Perce's voice came out of the shadows and made them jump. "But it also could possibly be an attempt to weaken our forces with a two front war. Fortunately, the space time continuum likes to be repaired, not unnaturally ripped open. We just have to keep it that way long enough."

"Long enough for what, for Dwendol to be evacuated so Reyortsed can take over it, his own planetary headquarters?" Gemini said, with that smile of hers that held no humor. "The Fairies and Elves would sooner die than see their world, everything they built, be lost to him."

Bennie had barely had time to finally register the fact Gemini was literally from another planet before Perce spoke again.

"Hopefully that won't happen, but they understand it may be inevitable to protect Pelanca," He said slowly, watching Gemini intently as she paled with a realization Bennie could not yet understand.

"How long?" Gemini said.

"A year, more or less," Perce said. "And that's about all the time I have left to train you guys. All the Guardians are going to be needed to combat Reyortsed's forces when the time comes, so you have to be ready."

Chapter Fifteen, Practice Problems

Bennie's summer began to pass too fast for her liking in a blur of visits to SeaWorld and Fiesta Texas with her friends, soccer practice, and summer reading during the day, followed by intense training at night, with a little sleep to keep her energy levels high. Bennie had little time to stop and think about what was going on. She just had to be ready for it.

Perce wasn't instructed to teach Bennie or her peers basic hand-to-hand combat or battle tactics, so he focused mainly on specific skills training, ethics, and tried to pound into their heads what measures could and could not be taken in hostile situations. Bennie went home every night with words milling in her head: "Don't accept a negotiation proposal that requires you to go somewhere alone and unarmed." "We don't leave people behind if there's a chance to get them to safety." "If you're responsible for a group of people it's always good to assign duties to others in the group with leadership skills. It saves your charge from mistakes you'd make by yourself and helps balance power, if not bring harmony. But be sure of who you pick to help lead."

Bennie's skills training kept her at a distance from Perce, Sean and Gemini, just as Gemini required a sound-proof shield wall while she worked on what Bennie called "the Siren trick." Gemini was composing the magical music made famous by the god-race her father came from. The music combined words and spells of a distracting and seductive nature into the enchanting melodies Gemini weaved on her small, harp-like instrument, called a *deron,* which was an Elven instrument she learned to play from her mother. Even Gemini's self-called "amateur racket" was strong enough to hypnotize Sean and even Bennie without the barrier. Perce was the only one with resistance training to the tactics Gemini was learning, and since he heard her songs in development it would be hardest for her to make his guard drop. When she succeeded, Perce would remove the sound proof shield and teach Sean and Bennie how to resist her music at full power, as they might face it against an enemy.

"It's taking longer than I'd hoped," Gemini said grimly when Perce dropped the barrier to check up on her. "I just don't feel the sorrow I'm supposed to feel as I 'reach desperately into the void for a comforting hand.'"

"Maybe you should write lyrics that match something you have felt, or are feeling, instead, so you can pull them through with true emotion you've experienced," Perce told her, "The girl in your song lost her source of strength and is looking for someone else to help her along. As far as I know your source of strength is in yourself, not an external being, and you haven't lost that strength, so the girl in the song is an outsider to you, not you yourself."

The rest of their conversation was lost as Perce put the sound barrier back up around them and listened to her within the walls of silence. Bennie glanced at Sean and grinned when she noticed the way he was avidly watching Gemini sing through the barrier. It was plain on his face he wanted to hear her.

Bennie's quiet laughter brought him to his senses and he tried his shape shifting practices again as Bennie, at her safe distance, tried to master the shotgun technique Esla had displayed that day in Pelanca, but the lightning still came pouring out of her hand in steady streams of electricity.

Another glance at Sean told Bennie he wasn't having much luck either. He was attempting to transform into a werewolf again but his mind must have only been half on the task at hand because only the upper half of him was transforming into the hairy, toothy nightmare, and the overall result was not intimidating in the slightest. Bennie hid behind the curtain of her hair to prevent Sean from seeing her tears of mirth. She got up and tapped on the side of the barrier to get Perce's attention and pointed at Sean as he re-morphed into his normal self. Perce dropped the barrier again to see what was up.

"Perce!" Sean said.

"Sean!" Perce replied in the exact same tone.

"I need your help."

Perce moved toward Sean, bringing up the sound barrier behind him. Only then did Bennie realize a strange, haunting echo had been resonating around the room, sobering her up, and had been cut off once the sound shield came up again. She raised her eyebrows at Gemini, who shrugged sheepishly. She had forgotten to stop her deron strings.

"What's up, Sean?" Perce was saying. Bennie half listened to the conversation while she built up electricity to project. *Maybe if I build up more charge it will be more likely to blast in spurts...*

"I can't get my legs to transform," Sean said, exasperated. "I don't get it."

"Sean," Perce said, "How many times do I have to tell you, *be the werewolf.* You're resisting the change because you aren't letting the thought be your one and only desire. I know it may not be the sexiest form you can have, but you have to want it to get it."

And if I can just get this release and retract concept I was picking up to work...

"I do want it, and I *am* being the werewolf, just half of me isn't cooperating!"

Bennie realized overcharging her arm was a bad idea a second too late. The built up power surge was too strong for her to retract. It was about to explode in every direction.

"WATCH OUT!" Bennie screamed, jerking her arm as far from her friends as she could just as the explosion of lightning illuminated the entire area and set their hair standing on end, crackling. The direct beam of lightning swept across the wall as Bennie spun it away and to her dismay it blasted right down an opening in the courtyard wall, past the back of the cafeteria building, and blasted into the main power generator of the school complex. Bennie blinked as the charge lit up the entire wiring and power lines around the school and stared in horror as the charges spread up every connection down the road, up the road-

-away...

Away...

Away.

The city kept going darker and darker in chunks. Bennie felt herself marveling that she could hold such an electric shock in her thin little arm.

Perce shot like a rocket to the school roof, then the water tower beyond the baseball field. He was a barely visible silhouette on the tower as the city continued to black out.

Ten seconds later Bennie could see him coming back down, but he was too far for her to see his expression. Before he got close enough, Bennie saw him snap his fingers or some other similar gesture, and all the lights in the entire city came back on instantaneously. He was close by then and Bennie saw his face ridiculously clearly.

He was just staring at her, his expression stuck between shock and amusement.

"San Antonio Split Second Blackout, anyone?" He said, the laughter clear in his voice. Bennie just stared in shock at her hand.

"You pack a power surge," Perce said, still grinning, but his voice was more serious now. "Don't worry, we'll work on avoiding this kind of thing, it's awfully dangerous. What were you doing?"

"I really don't know," Bennie said, "It's all so trial and error, I had no clue I could do that. Or that that was what would happen."

"Tell me about it," Gemini said as she shut off the barrier-her deron strings stopped properly this time. "I've worked with *Sean*, and that still freaked me out!"

"Ouch, that wasn't very nice," Sean said with a mock-offended expression. Bennie relaxed a little.

"At least I know now that it's a bad idea to over power myself-no pun intended," Bennie said as Sean let out a "ha-ha."

"Not always a bad idea," Perce said, "That type of surge could be useful against a powerful foe, but you need to learn to control it. Either way, we'd better quit for the night in case someone says they saw the surge originate from here and people come looking. I'll walk you home."

* * *

There was plenty about the blackout on the news, plenty about how no one (but Bennie and her friends) could figure out what had happened or where it had begun. There were no witnesses, none who came forward at least.

There had been one other pair of eyes viewing the incident, a pair of black eyes peering from a darkened corner of a roof top, where only Bennie would have seen him, had she looked that way.

He knew he shouldn't have gone out unprotected, but the powerful protective charms and spells would have taken long to prepare, and the attention they would have drawn would have made it harder for him to escape in secret.

He wanted to see this Shadowchild himself, without Gregk attempting an attact. The demon could have his revenge at another time.

That girl will indeed be a force to be reckoned with, but she's nothing yet. I'll have to assign someone to her, but not tonight. Reyortsed pushed his long black hair from his face, lifted himself up gracefully, and silently slipped away to the rend he'd made undetected and vanished.

* * *

Bennie slipped quietly into the house after the classic group hug, and bumped right into her cousin.

"Hey, Tim!" She said, "What are you doing out so late?"

"I was about to say the same to you," Bennie's mother gave her a suspicious look. "You said you'd be staying at Sarah's for the night, you can't seriously have walked home all by yourself."

"Her brother brought me back when the lights went out," Bennie said, wishing she didn't have to lie. "We thought it was just their block. If we'd known the lights were back on already…"

"*All* the power went out so we came over. But it's back on now." Tim said, and made a face that showed he was rather disappointed with that fact. "I wanted it to stay off so we could roast marshmallows like we did during that nasty storm that one time."

"Who says we can't?" Bennie said. Tim looked at her hopefully, then at Bennie's mom and aunt.

"As long as it's at the table," Judy, Bennie's aunt, said. "That okay with you, Bonnie?"

"Well, maybe one marshmallow each, or two," Bennie's mom said. "You can stay the night if you want."

"No, we'll be heading back. Eric's on business and I don't like to leave our house empty at night."

Tim returned with a bag of marshmallows and the skewers while Bennie's mom relit the candles and Bennie pretended to go call Sarah so she'd know Bennie got home safe.

As Bennie watched her marshmallow bubble and brown over the candle flame after faking the call, she wondered if she could produce fire as powerfully as she had the lightning.

I'd probably set off an explosion that'd kill everyone if I ever tried.

Chapter Sixteen, Secrets

"The girl's power is already massive. Not even her father could do what she did tonight," Reyortsed paced slowly past Gregk the demon, concealing his true opinions with a cool and collected demeanor. "It is remarkable that such strength should develop over such a small stretch of time. Had you crossed her path now instead of when you did you wouldn't have survived.

"I consider myself lucky, then," growled the demon in his gravelly and ancient voice. "She's more than she knows, which makes her even more dangerous than if she did, since the Guardians place ethics above a quick victory."

"Intuitive as always, my friend," Reyortsed said, pressing his fingers against his shoulder. "Excuse me a moment."

Reyortsed guided his strong and slender frame gracefully out the door into his private chambers before allowing himself an irritated grimace of pain, angered by his own weakness.

I should be able to handle this better, but it only gets worse. Reyortsed reached out a shaking hand and grasped a bottle of ointment from behind a secret panel. He ripped his shirt away from his shoulder and began rubbing the foul-smelling solution into the strange birthmark on his shoulder that had given him pain for years.

No, not pain. I know *pain, better than most. This is different, like a part of me fighting another to the death.*

The strange pain was numbed now and Reyortsed went to pull on his shirt, but instead traced the red and angry mark with his finger:

P

Suddenly, something in his mind clicked.

* * *

The mark on Bennie's shoulder tingled with an itch as she walked along through Pelanca. At the same time she reached to scratch at it, she noticed Perce going for the matching tattoo on his finger. If he had seen her look, he did a good job of pretending not to notice.

What the heck was that all about?

She stopped to buy a bracelet on her way out that matched her moonstone necklace.

"Very nice," Perce said as Gemini helped Bennie clasp the bracelet on. "We'll have to go sightseeing in Pelanca one of these days, and go to the beach."

"I'm just glad that in Pelanca they take any currency and exchange it for you instead of-What beach?" Bennie said.

Shadowchild

"You didn't think Pelanca City was all there was to this world, did you?" Perce grinned. "Yeah, so only this Island is known-no one has ever come back from sailing to the horizon on the silver seas, but it's a nice vacation spot for Guardians."

"I'm so gone!" Bennie said, "I live 3 hours from the Gulf Coast and I haven't seen sand for over four years!"

"We'll put that on the agenda," Sean said, putting his arm around Gemini, "Who wants to bet how many heads our Gem will turn in a string bikini?"

Gemini pushed his arm away, "Lemur!" she said.

"Oh! You never did explain that myth to me," Bennie said. "So what's 'Lemur' mean?"

The only response she got back was laughter, but it was caught short when they noticed some groups of Guardians running and shouting.

"Whoa! Marek!" Perce shouted into the air, "What the hell happened?"

"It's *him,*" The winged man Bennie had seen soared above the growing crowd.

God that's awesome, Bennie thought.

"He sent some trouble makers through a rend in Texas. We could use your help if you can spare it."

"Texas?" Bennie panicked, "Perce, do you think…?"

"It's too early to tell yet, I have to go with them," Perce said.

"We're going too, then," Sean said firmly, but Perce shook is head.

"I need you all to go straight to Aila's and stay there."

"Perce!"

"Sean, you understand this isn't the right time, and you're the only one out of you three with any battle experience and so you have to take care of them! Please don't argue with me."

131

Bennie noticed Perce seemed way too worried. This couldn't be any normal skirmish.

"Perce," her voice sounded small. He smiled at her.

"I'll stay out of trouble," Perce said, "But right now you need to get to Aila and stay out of trouble too. She'll take care of you guys while I'm gone."

"Perce-" Gemini said, but Perce had already vanished into the masses. Sean, clearly unhappy, took charge.

"Well, we heard him, let's get out of here."

* * *

Bennie was only unnerved even more by how livid Aila was when she learned Perce had run off. She went on muttering for two very long hours about Perce having bigger responsibilities. She checked in on the three of them repeatedly and gave them some strange food Bennie had never eaten before, but would have found tasty had she not been sick with worry.

As the third hour passed since they had arrived at Aila's the fairy started pacing quietly, eyes darting at every sound. Bennie was beginning to get very scared, and Gemini had noticed.

"He'll be fine, Bennie. Perce has been in worse," she said, but Bennie knew she only half believed what she was saying.

They sat in silence after that for a long time. Bennie rubbed her shoulder.

"You've been doing that a lot since we got here," Sean said. "Did you hurt yourself?"

"I don't know," Bennie said, drawing her arm away. "I didn't know I was doing it."

"Let me have a look," Aila said, "Just for the sake of having something to do." She gently pushed Bennie's collar back off her shoulder next to her collarbone. She stopped, looking very awkward suddenly.

"Sean, Gemini, would you go out and see if anything is happening outside? Don't go too far."

After the two had gone with confused looks on their faces, Aila gently traced her finger over Bennie's strange new mark. "That came with the lightning strike, no?"

Bennie nodded.

"I should have realized that was it. Sorry, I'm silly. It should stop hurting on it's own but I'll give you some solution for the next time it bothers you."

"It's not painful," Bennie said, "It's different, like… a part of me is being tugged in two different directions… by chains centered on top of the mark...or something…"

Aila looked at Bennie thoughtfully, but snapped out of her reverie at the sound of the front door being kicked open.

Bennie jerked her collar up and jumped up, gasping with relief and horror.

"Holy crap, Perce!" she said, hugging him then examining his bloodied face.

" 'Tis but a scratch," Perce said in a very good Monty Python impersonation as Sean and Gemini both tried to clean the slashes on the side of his face.

"I think that's more than a scratch, mister," Aila snapped, "And since I'm the healer we'll go by what I say. What the hell were you thinking, running off like that? You've got more important things on your hands to look out for than some bloody rend!"

Perce was plunked down forcefully into a chair while Aila started treating his injuries.

"It was really bad, Aila, and you know I couldn't stay without raising suspicion."

"Hmph," Aila snorted as the gashes on Perce's face vanished without a trace under her hand.

"But we got them in the end," Perce said, the smile in his voice if not in his immobilized face, "And-"

"I DON'T CARE!" Aila shouted. "*YOU'VE* Got to be careful now! He's caught on, Perce. Why do you think that attack was set up?"

"We'll discuss this later," Perce said, sounding unusually grave.

"Perce," Sean jumped in, "What's this about?"

"Something Aila shouldn't be letting you all worry about right now," Perce said, shooting the fairy a warning look. "But I do need to tell you that the attack *was* in San Antonio."

"What?" Gemini said. Bennie paled.

"No one was badly hurt, memories are being rewritten and the mess is being cleaned up," Perce said. "But we're going to have to train in Pelanca from now on. We can't afford to be caught off guard during practice."

The group sat in silence for a moment before Bennie spoke up.

"So they were after *us?*"

She almost said "me" because she could tell nothing this drastic had happened to the group before she arrived, but she didn't want to sound overly paranoid.

Perce looked her deep in the eyes.

"I don't want you to worry–any of you," he said. "But I won't lie to you."

Bennie sighed. She *would* worry. If Reyortsed was concerned about them, or her, he could hurt her family, blood family and this new family she was now part of. She couldn't bear to lose any of them.

"I'll be staying in my apartment here so I'll show you where it is," Perce said. "Sean, I expect you to pick up Bennie every night we train and come straight here. Take the larger tunnels so you can fly. Absolutely no going anywhere alone for either of you, check your back and make sure no one is following best as you can. Gem, you come with one of the groups from Dwendol. We'll meet at my place at ten thirty each night."

Aila saw them to the door, hovering at eye level with Perce. She cupped his face in her hand.

"I'm sorry I yelled at you," she said. "I was just scared, you understand. Do try to stay out of trouble now?"

"I already am," Perce smiled at her. Then he followed his charge out the door.

* * *

Perce lived in a small, simple but tasteful apartment on the outskirts of Pelanca. Bennie couldn't help noticing that Perce's rooms, though certainly lived in, were very clean, despite the "all men are slobs" stereotype.

"Y'all hungry?" he said, pulling some TV dinners out of the freezer. Apparently he didn't cook much though. Bennie shifted on her feet.

"I don't think I could eat right now," she said.

"Me either," Gemini agreed.

"I'll take the teriyaki," Sean grinned, but the grin was forced. And Perce saw straight through it.

"Look, I know you guys are worried, but there's nothing to it right now."

"Then why is Reyortsed looking for us?" Sean spouted. "He's certainly something to it, if you ask me. He's the biggest threat to the Guardians since Sheyneh's time!"

Perce remained silent and expressionless. Bennie watched as Sean calculated something from Perce's face into his mind, before understanding lit up in his eyes.

"That's what this is all about, isn't it?" he said to Perce. Bennie was confused.

"I think we should call it a night," Perce said.

Chapter Seventeen, AIMing for Answers

Bennie talked to Sean over AOL Instant Messenger later that night. Neither could shake off what had happened to them.

BenJ09: Sheyneh was the powerful shape shifter who saved the Guardians right? Perce mentioned her to me once.

HadrianSF7: Totally. No one's more important in Guardian History.

BenJ09: So what does she have to do with the present situation?

HadrianSF7: SC, you know about Sheyneh's other power, right?

BenJ09: ??

HadrianSF7: Sheyneh had some sort of power-persuasiveness or something-could manipulate people into seeing her POV-very effective and dangerous. That's why she kicked @$$-she had the perfect mindset.

BenJ09: That is a pretty dangerous power-wrong person with that ability could ruin things for everyone.

HadrianSF7: Seems to already be happening. I'm pretty sure that Reyortsed has that same sort of power-but people don't talk about him much. Bad table conversation.

BenJ09: This whole Guardian business keeps getting better. Crap, Sean. Reyortsed can twist people?

HadrianSF7: I'm beginning to think so after tonight.

BenJ09: y?

HadrianSF7: You heard of the prophecy yet?

BenJ09: What Perce told me.

HadrianSF7: J.A.S.

Sean spent his "just a second" in quiet typing for a while so Bennie switched over to talk with her friend Sarah. They opened a chat with Bennie and Sarah's other friends Natalie and Jacob.

Jak0Bad: Been working-not been on a lot since school got out

Taken360: It's Sarah, new sn. Welcome back.

Natsdb0mb: HIIIII!!!!

Taken360: Bennie where r u tonight we usually can't get a type in edgewise when you start but you're quiet.

BenJ09: Talking to someone.

Natsdb0mb: who?

Bennie saw Sean's AIM window flash orange. He had entered text.

BenJ09: brb

HadrianSF7: Here's the prophecy in total:

For an age Sheyneh's peace shall reign strong and will keep,

The force of evil at bay

But what hides in the darkness will wake from it's sleep

And spill to the light of day

And a son of Sheyneh shall be stolen away,

Taking many for his own,

And the wings of scarlet shall rise up once again

To claim his abandoned throne.

For the light shall lead those who are lost in the night

Back to their home in the day

The forces of dark and light shall clash once again.

And each will keep theirs and stay.

HadrianSF7: So u c

HadrianSF7: Reyortsed Must be the "Son of Sheyneh" which means his rival is coming-or may even be here already. But what Perce was trying to keep us cool about that I figured out was happening is that we're alive during the prophecy.

BenJ09: So who's the rival if the time is right?

HadrianSF7: Perce knows. It's obvious. Maybe Esla…whoa hey! Maybe it's PERCE! Maybe that's why our group is being targeted-Reyortsed must have figured it out!

BenJ09: No way. Perce? I dunno.

HadrianSF7: Why else would Reyortsed pay so much attention to us?

BenJ09: I dunno but th-

Taken360: BOO!

BenJ09: re's gotta be another explanation.

Bennie had pressed enter before she realized a new window had popped up and taken most of her reply to Sarah instead of Sean.

BenJ09: Ahh! Sarah!

Taken360: Chica where r u? What needs another explanation?

BenJ09: Sorry, important convo-brb.

Taken360:…

Bennie copied and pasted the rest of her sentence into Sean's window then typed:

BenJ09: Sean I'll bbs-my friends are getting suspicious of how much time I'm spending on this convo.

HadrianSF7: Gotya.

BenJ09: I'll make another sn so this doesn't happen too much.

HadrianSF7: No worries SC. I am being called for anyway, by the pillow. Not slept for about 3 weeks now.

BenJ09: get out! I can go only 4-5 days! Perce was bad enough with two months!

HadrianSF7: You get better at it-upshot of being a Guardian. :-P

HadrianSF7: Yo!

HadrianSF7 signed off at 2:54 pm.

Bennie turned back to the chat-which had filled with miles of multicolored text.

BenJ09: Back, sorry. Important convo.

Taken360: musta been *evil grin*

Jak0Bad: Who with?

BenJ09: buddy of mine-name is Sean.

Natsdb0mb: ooohhhhh :-*

BenJ09: NO not like that-he likes someone else n e ways.

Jak0Bad: so it's still the one and only Marcus for you? :-P

BenJ09: Be nice >:-P

Bennie signed off as quickly as possible, went to aim.com and made a new screen name: Shadowchild7. Simple enough. Her night name plus her favorite number and voila! She and Sean could talk without further interruptions. Sadly he was offline.

I'll have to get Gemini a screen name so we can all talk without anyone popping in on us.

Bennie hadn't bargained on the fact "popping in" on her would be only a few clicks away for a computer hacker who was already watching her every move.

His real name was Christopher Quinten, but he was better known as ICU3000 by people who needed a spy. Bennie knew nothing about him, but many others did, and had she known them she'd know he was trouble, and if he was looking her up for someone she could be sure she was in trouble.

Christopher typed into his own AIM window:

<u>ICU3000:</u> I have your chick, Mr. R. She has a new screen name: Shadowchild7. Should I trace the computer?

<u>Mr. R:</u> No need to go that far yet. I just needed to be sure we had the right girl.

Christopher began to feel a bit drowsy and heard the next words instead of saw them on the computer screen:

I'll contact you if I need you again. Remember, no bragging about me to your friends, and be sure to wipe your system clean of our history.

"Yeah..." Christopher muttered out loud before mechanically removing anything that might prove he'd been in contact with his newest client, and then falling asleep.

He'd better have the money coming...lame loser, can't even keep his girlfriend from blocking him and not giving out her new screen name...

Buzzz.

Christopher jumped awake. Why he was asleep at his computer was beyond him.

Buzzz.

He grabbed his vibrating cell phone from the charger on the floor. It was his mom. He quickly made ready his busy college student ruse and ignored the creepy feeling he had about not being able to remember the past several hours very well at all.

Chapter Eighteen, Friends

Bennie turned up for training with Sean the next night, but Sean said before they made their way to Perce's apartment he needed to return a video game to a friend.

"This friend lives in Pelanca?" Bennie said.

"No, but he's training in Pelanca with another group. He was the rookie until about a little while ago; this girl who joined their group can communicate with insects. I think she's the one Esla mentioned when we saw him. My friend says bees are her favorite, and that she's really strange."

"Hmm," Bennie said, wondering why it had never occurred to her there were other little groups being trained outside her own. It wasn't like she hadn't seen people being trained in Pelanca before.

It was not long before Sean and Bennie reached their destination: a large park with open, grassy fields perfect for football games and Guardian training. There was a strong looking Centaur woman there, parrying fiery spells from a small, dark-haired elf while a boy about Bennie's age with dirty blonde hair fiddled with something glittering in his hands. A buzzing lump on the ground became a small figure swarming with bees when Bennie and Sean got closer.

Suddenly the bees darted away from the figure on the ground and surrounded Sean and Bennie.

" It's just friendly curiosity," said a familiar voice from the other side, "They won't sting if you don't attack them."

"Or unless you tell them to!" said another voice that Bennie assumed belonged to the boy, since it was male. The bees buzzed away and Bennie received a shock when she saw the round face smiling at her from beneath them.

"Rachel!" Bennie said.

Rachel was Sarah's little sister, who'd be coming to high school at the end of August. Bennie knew her almost as well as she knew her best friend since the two sisters were almost always in the house at the same time.

"Esla told me you were a Guardian too when he found out you knew my sister. I couldn't wait to surprise you!"

"She does carry the element of surprise," the boy said.

"Oh hush, you!" Rachel said and the swarm of bees swirled together to form the letters "shh" between them. Bennie laughed.

"Not to cut the reunion short," Sean said with genuine regret in his voice. "We were just stopping by before training to give you back your copy of Halo 2." Sean handed his friend the game. "And I think introductions are in order since only Bennie and Rachel know each other. Bennie, this is Peter."

"Ah, Benjamina!" Peter said with an exaggerated bow, "Such a pleasure. Sean speaks of you often!"

"Does he?" Bennie said, giving Sean a "did you put him up to this?" look.

"Well, not as often as he speaks of one Gemini," Peter said, straightening himself again, "But he did mention that your eyes are the loveliest shade of grey."

Rachel rolled her eyes.

"*All* of our eyes are grey, Petes. It's part of the Guardian group fashion."

"Please excuse the strange blonde girl in black," Peter said, continuing his ruse. "Could I interest you in a diamond-a diamond ring perhaps?"

Peter uncurled his hand dramatically and Bennie saw a good sized rock in his palm shape itself into a flat band-literally a *diamond ring.*

"Peter manipulates diamonds," Rachel and Sean both said in unison.

"A fact he enjoys using to pretend he's God's gift to women," the lady centaur said, trotting over.

"He seems to have it down to an art form," Bennie responded, crossing her arms and raising an eyebrow at Peter. He closed his fist around the diamond and pocketed it.

"No," he said, becoming a normal human being again, "Having it down to an art form would require removing these pests from the scene." He grinned as he gestured at his comrades. "But it is nice to meet you either way."

"You too," Bennie said, shaking his hand. "I *would* like a diamond ring but I don't want to take from your supply."

Peter laughed. "Wise," he said. "I get my supply from the dwarves and they're particular about me not losing them too easily. I can make them change shape, size, density, even substance. I simply rearrange the molecular structure to do that. The drawback is once it's no longer a diamond I can't control it, so I can't change it back. So I avoid doing that."

"The dwarves would have my haunches if I let him waste their stones," the lady centaur said. "His ability is usually only found in their kind, and it's still a rare gift."

"Having a skill that usually belongs within the racial boundaries of the dwarves does lead me to the conclusion I had a dwarf ancestor or two," Peter said. "That would explain why I'm short."

"You're not short," Bennie said, sizing up Peter's frame. He wasn't as tall as Sean but he was at least five foot six. She was a little less than eye-level with him.

"Yes I am," Peter said, "But anyway, you haven't been introduced to Jinx-real name Erlina-"

"Who's the REAL short one here," said the petite elf. Up close she looked to be in her early twenties by human years, but was probably a lot older. Unlike Gemini, who glowed with glorious beauty from both halves of her heritage, Erlina caught your attention by being a flicker in the corner of your eye. She was small with a mischievous face and short, black hair. She was about three inches shorter than Rachel, at shoulder height to Peter. She moved as nimbly and swiftly as a cat.

"Everyone on my mother's side of the family is small," she said, pushing her fringe of dark hair out of her eyes. "Just genetics it seems. It can come in handy though. Oh, I tend to go by Jinx because Erlina is a very common name in my family, but you can call me either."

"I like Jinx, and it's nice to meet you as well," Bennie said.

"You can call me Karla, or Fleta if you prefer Night Names," the lady centaur said. "As for Jinx, don't be fooled by her fun-loving impressions," she smiled. "She's the biggest fan of no-nonsense training I've ever met."

"Is that a compliment?" Jinx's eyebrows shot up and her lips quirked into an almost threatening, yet obviously amused semi-pucker.

"Yes," Peter said, "But they did have to assign me with you to give you a bit of a sense of humor."

"Like this?" Jinx blinked at Peter and his hair turned a bright, hot pink with blue strips zigzagging across the sides. Bennie burst out laughing.

"Yes, like that," Peter said, "Now change it back, please? My mom will freak if she sees this!"

"Maybe later," Jinx said over her shoulder. Rachel buried herself under the cloud of bees to hide her face, reddening with suppressed laughter.

"You still alive in there?" Bennie said to Rachel. "You haven't told me how you got here, or what your night name is."

"Reyna," Rachel said as the bees cleared from her face, "Means Queen, like the bee queen? You know?"

Bennie nodded.

"I got hit by the lightning not long after you did but no one saw-in my family at least. One of the Guardians showed up and told me what had happened to me and I saw that he was right about the insects and not sleeping, and he sort of helped me figure myself out before I came to Pelanca and met Fleta and Jinx and Peter, and it all took off from there."

"When I tried to pull my charming man with a diamond role on her she loosed a swarm of mosquitoes on me," Peter said. "I'll never be able to donate blood due to the risk that I have malaria now."

"Seriously, Petes. Not a single one of those mosquitoes bit you. I'm not that cruel."

"Just like to use that as my excuse to avoid needles!"

"And Peter doesn't like to mention that his Night Name is Mason, so I will for him!" Rachel said gleefully. Peter groaned.

"I like the name Mason, I really do," he said, "But my brother *and* my cousin *and* one of my friends all have that name so you give it to me and I can't think of who I am!"

"Someone needs their head looked at," Fleta the Centaur smiled.

"You see? You see Sean?" Peter said in mock distress, "I *told* you the nonstop picking on me only got worse when Rachel showed up!"

"You need another guy in your group," Sean grinned.

They had reached the edge of the field, so Sean and Bennie made their goodbyes and headed toward Perce's.

"Nice bunch of people," Bennie said to Sean.

"Yeah," Sean said, watching a Leweline swoop overhead. "I think Peter likes you."

"Yeah, right," Bennie said, and knocked on Perce's door.

It was the end of July, and soccer practice was pausing. Bennie returned home from her last practice, stripped down to her waist and sprawled flat on the floor under her ceiling fan. No better way to cool off while waiting for the shower to be available.

The phone rang. Groaning, Bennie rolled over and pulled on a shirt, buttoning it as she darted down the stairs to answer it.

"206? I don't recognize that area code," Bennie said to herself, waiting for the answering machine to pick up.

Hey, Bennie, it's Sean-

-And Peter!

-Sean and Peter and we're-

"Hello?" Bennie picked up. "Sorry, I didn't recognize the area code."

"That's because we're in Seattle," Sean said, laughing.

"*Seattle?*" Bennie said. "What are you doing in Seattle?"

"Peter *lives* in Seattle!" Sean replied. Bennie could hear Peter laughing in the background.

"Okay...so how did he end up in Pelanca the other night?"

"The same way we did of course!" Sean said. "Did you think everyone you saw was a local San Antonian? Gem's from an entirely different galaxy, you know."

Bennie heard Peter say something about that being why only someone as weird as Sean was attracted to her. Sean promptly told him to shut up, but Bennie heard the amusement in his voice.

"So the *reason* we were calling," Sean said, "is that Pete and I are bored out of our brains and want to have a World of Warcraft tournament, but we need more nerds. Gem doesn't play these games and we have a couple of Pete's friends, here and online, but we thought you might be interested.

"I've never played World of Warcraft," Bennie said. "Not to mention I don't think my mom would appreciate me gallivanting off to Seattle."

"Just tell your mom you're going to your friend's house for the day!" Peter said. "We'll teach you how to play."

"That rhymed," a strange voice said from a distance. "Peter's a poet!"

"Shut up, Mason." Peter said, evidently over his shoulder, before turning back to the phone. "So how about it? Sean will come over and show you which way to Seattle from Pelanca and-"

"You guys!" Bennie said laughing. "I just got off soccer practice! I'm sweaty! I *stink.* And after I have my shower I'd have to blow dry my hair before I could go anywhere because it likes to frizz."

"Trifles!" Sean said. "We're all guys over here! Not to mention we're playing a war game and in a real battle none of us would care if we stunk."

"Or we could just have someone come show up at your house and get you hooked up so you can play from there," Peter remarked. "But it's more fun to throw popcorn at each other when we're in the same room instead of sending cyber missiles across the United States. And it costs money to play online."

"I think I should probably go over there, but does it have to be tonight?" Bennie asked. "I don't have practice after today so I could come around some other night when I was fit for a pretend war."

"Well, if you insist on leaving us one man short," Sean said into the phone.

"One *woman* short," Bennie corrected him.

"Ok, one woman. We'll let you know ahead of time when we do this again-which is about every afternoon, even during school. It's addictive, can you tell?"

"Works for me," Bennie said. "I'll talk to you later."

"Bye!" Four different voices called from the phone.

"What? Am I on speaker?" Bennie asked.

"Yeah," Peter said, mirth in his voice. "So you told four very hot single high school guys you're stinky and sweaty!"

"OOOOHHHH!!!" The others said, save for Sean who was remarking he was actually going into college.

"Very funny," Bennie said, not really offended, and hung up.

Chapter Nineteen, World of Warcraft

"I still don't know why I'm doing this with you guys," Bennie said the next afternoon as she drove with Sean to the entry point they took to Pelanca since he needed to fly them there himself. "I don't even play video games."

"*Computer* games," Sean corrected, "*World of Warcraft* is a computer game, and you're playing it with us because we men are very persuasive, and you have a gamer inside you somewhere that's subconsciously dying to get out and beat the crap out of some newbies."

"I *am* a newbie, Sean," Bennie said, "I've never done it before and I'm going to get creamed."

"*Pwned* is the correct term," Sean said.

"Pwned?"

"Lesson one in gaming: When someone beats someone else, completely whips their ass, they'd say "I owned you" or something like that. Well, somewhere someone or several someones made a typo: pwned. And it just stuck, I guess. That's my theory at least."

"Ookaaayy…" Bennie said under her breath.

They parked in the lot outside Raymond Rimkus Park. Bennie followed Sean down into the shallow gully around the park. There was no water in it during this time of year, and their feet crunched on the rocks as they crawled into a draining tunnel.

They followed the tunnel and suddenly were in the wide open tunnel to Pelanca. Sean waited for another something-or-other to fly by before grabbing Bennie, jumping into the open space and transforming into the gargoyle in mid-air.

He flew them carefully down into the caverns of Pelanca then around into another tunnel. They went up until they emerged into a bunch of trees on a hillside overlooking a small neighborhood nestled around a lake.

Bennie was stunned by how different everything looked here. For one thing it was much *greener* than anything she had seen before, and the trees were mostly needle-bearing, unlike the live oaks she was used to. The air felt very soft and cool, almost like a phantom liquid, and Bennie wondered at how this could possibly be summertime.

The sky differed most of all, though. Bennie had heard rumors that around Seattle it never stopped raining, but today was the exception, for the little blue patch stuck on top of the drastic hills was a true blue, not the remarkable turquoise Bennie knew at home.

"What do you think?" Sean said. "Different isn't it?"

"Where are we?" Bennie said, looking at the absurd amount of green.

"We're in Seattle…well, technically Silverdale, which is a pretty good ferry-ride from Seattle but you'd have no idea what I was talking about if I said Silverdale.

"It's nice," Bennie said, shivering slightly in the oddly cool air. "Smells better than San Antonio, but it's awfully cool for summer."

"Peter thinks San Antonio is hotter than hell!" Sean laughed. "Amazing the difference a few hundred miles can make."

They scurried down the hill to the curving streets with their homes nestled in the trees. The golden sunlight made them look greener than ever, but Bennie didn't have time to admire the scenery before she was ushered into one of the houses by Peter and his friends.

"So! Intro!" Peter said. "You know Sean, and me, so this is Mason-my cousin, Mason-my brother, and Mason-my friend, Rick, and Josh."

Bennie failed to hide her amusement as he pointed out the three Masons. She would be able to remember which one was his brother-they looked so much alike-but she had to pound into her head that the white blond, tall and skinny Mason was his cousin, and the copper-haired muscle man was his pal. Rick and Josh weren't hard to remember; Rick had black hair and dark skin, and Josh was fair as a ghost with freckles and green eyes.

"Guys," Peter continued, "This is the lovely Benjamina, who came all the way from San Antonio with Sean."

"So you guys know I'm not from around here then?" Bennie said, wondering that none of them found it odd she had crossed the country in a matter of minutes.

"Well, it's hard to keep your Guardian status from your twin and your rooming cousin," Peter said, "Especially when they're as nocturnal as you. Rick and I met in Pelanca, and when you have two best friends like Josh and Mason no.3 it's no fun to lie to them."

"I'm glad he finally did come around and tell me what the heck was going on," Josh remarked. "I thought he'd robbed a jewel shop when he pulled that diamond out of his pocket and was totally lost when he made it morph into a knife. Once I knew we couldn't leave our pal Mason in the dark."

"Whoa, why did you need a knife?" Bennie said worriedly.

"Some freaky critter was about to kill a fellow Guardian," Peter said, his quick glance at Sean did not go unnoticed by Bennie, but something in Peter's voice said he'd rather not talk about it, so she didn't press the matter further.

"So you've never played World of Warcraft?" Rick said. "Well we'd better get started. There's a lot of material to cover and not enough time."

"Have a seat," Mason–Peter's brother– said as he moved from his spot at the computer. The boys crowded around after Bennie was set in front of the screen.

"So Bennie," Peter said as he opened the program and signed himself on. "World of Warcraft, or WOW, is a simulated online role-playing game made up of several levels. Every time you kill something, you gain experience and are closer to progressing to the next level."

"Great," Bennie said. *Now I get to be a world wide web murderer.*

"But," Sean interjected, "You start at the very bottom. Basically everything is above you, and you can only kill something less experienced so you have to start out small, but you don't want to keep killing the same thing because you get less experience with every kill and eventually you outgrow whatever it is and have to progress to something harder."

Why I'm doing this I'll never know… Bennie thought.

"There's an experience gap of sorts," Rick continued. "Four levels below you and five above are where you can get the experience. But with ten levels above you you're pwned."

"That word again."

Everyone laughed.

"Now don't forget the color code," Peter said to her, leaning in to point at the screen. "Green means you get little experience, yellow means you'll get a decent amount, and red: you had better be good or you'll be dead."

"Peter rhymed again!" Cousin Mason chirped. "I think Bennie's romancing poetry out of him." Peter hit him.

"So *quests*," he said quickly. "You can look at a mission in a chatbox, like this one." He stopped at a camp and looked at the quest, and clicked decline. "You can accept or decline, but if you accept you have to go back to that person to get your experience. And if you succeed you get more than you would just goofing off, but we're goofing today since you're new to it."

"That's very sweet," Bennie said, not sure if she really believed it.

Peter stopped to kill something on the computer screen.

"You press the A-1 keys to fight," He said, killing the tiger. Bennie looked sadly at the dead computer creature. It seemed so pointless.

"After killing something there's loot to pick up sometimes," Josh said, "That shows up as little objects, but there's nothing to keep here except a ruined pelt."

The mental image made Bennie gag.

"And what is the point of this again?" She said, trying to hide her disgust to avoid offending her new friends. "You just kill?"

"Well it's not really the killing that's the point," Peter said, seeming to sense her discomfort. "It's to gain experience and to survive through the levels. At level forty you can even buy a mount. The gnomes have robot chickens, it's really funny."

Bennie smiled. That was a better image. But then she stared at the screen in shock.

"Is there a reason for you to be on fire?" She said.

"That's my shield." The boys laughed.

"Oh." Bennie blinked as Peter saved his game and began setting up one for her.

"Pick a race," he said, allowing her control of the mouse.

"Um," Bennie scanned the list. "I think I'll be a night elf."

She spent a few minutes creating her simulated self and got the game started.

"Okay here's the fun part," Twin Mason said, reaching over and clicking a few buttons. "Flirt lines."

All of a sudden Bennie's night elf spoke:

"Yes I have exotic piercings."

Bennie stared at her creation in shock. The explosion of laughter at the expression on her face went on for over a minute.

"She did not just say what I thought she said," Bennie said, her own laughter coming out.

"There's eight other races of those flirts you haven't heard yet!" Sean said, his face red as he began laughing so breathlessly it was a high-pitched squeak. Everyone started laughing again.

Bennie began working the keys and mouse to get her elf running. She was very clumsy at first and somehow managed to get stuck between a hill and a stone building.

"Looks like I'm stuck between a rock and a hard place!" Bennie said, laughing freely with the boys now.

Bennie decided to forgo actually killing anything for the time being, and managed promptly to get herself killed. As her wisp found its way back to her body Peter explained the different races and zones.

"I like the music," Bennie said once her elf was alive again.

Peter reached over and pressed some more keys. The elf began dancing. Bennie laughed.

"Each zone has it's own music and each race has its own dance," he explained. The elf was done dancing and Peter directed Bennie out of a corner she had run into–again.

"Going to kill anything to get experience yet or are you just going to run into corners?" Sean said, still breathless with laughter.

"Actually you probably should take me home now," Bennie said. "We've been here nearly two hours so my mom will be waiting for me to get back soon, and I'd rather not relive the other day."

"Oh yeah," Sean said, while the guys groaned. "I'll get on at home you guys and we'll play. We've got days enough to convert Bennie to our cult, no worries."

No worries that I'll ever do anything more than run into corners, Bennie grinned to herself. She had no stomach for killing, real or pretend, but today was priceless. She had plenty of stomach for laughing, especially with the goof troop she had found herself with.

Chapter Twenty, Puzzle Pieces

Bennie spent a lot of afternoons either in Sean's room talking online to her friends in Washington, or there in Silverdale herself. They laughed at her when she did occasionally play and get herself stuck, and she laughed when the guys jumped at the thunderstorm that hit one day (Save for Rick-who was from Florida, and Sean, naturally). They were used to the steady grey and quiet drizzles and got very excited when the thunder boomed. It echoed interestingly around the hills, unlike the solid grumbles Bennie heard at home almost every time it rained, when it actually did rain.

Peter proved to be a really good help with her computer movement skills, but she deliberately screwed up just to keep things fun, and to keep her need to start slaughtering things away. She got to laugh over the internet at some of the boys' other friends who lived all over.

Other times she spent just hanging around, watching movies or going over summer reading (the latter of which proved easier to work on when she was with Rachel and Sarah). Bennie found that she and Peter had a strangely similar taste in movies, and more than once they went to the theatre to "scout out" movies that would be good to rent later on.

Bennie marveled one night after practice that for the first summer in her life she hadn't suffered boredom once, and the end of summer was coming too quickly.

The next afternoon she and Peter were headed back to his house to deliver information on a new film to their new friends. They were discussing the finer points of the plot as they got off the bus and made their way down the street while they digressed into what Bennie always labeled as "dangerous territory": the love interests in the movie.

"I still think Anne was stupid for putting up with David for so long," Peter said. "With her capabilities she could have simply erased herself from his memory and been done with him. I was glad that she finally gave up on him and pursued her potential with mind manipulation. Maybe she'll turn out evil in the sequel."

"She was *trying* to give him a chance," Bennie argued. "Girls don't give up on guys so easily, even if we don't stalk them or anything."

"Oh really?" Peter said, giving her a sideways smile. "Anyone you're holding out for?"

Bennie thought of the past school year. She remembered that first chemistry lab, when she was ready to explode with the chemicals. Her lab partner Marcus had saved the day. He had done so for every lab they had together, her personal grade-saver...

"They were only minor characters anyways," Bennie quickly got them back on track with the movie. "I think that our friends will find the main plot of the film more interesting-"

Peter suddenly threw Bennie onto the ground and rolled them behind a bunch of trashcans.

"Ow?" Bennie said when he rolled off her. Her elbow was bleeding and her jeans were ripped, revealing more blood. *Wonderful. Now I look trendy, but I'll have a scar peeking through the hole.*

"Sorry Bennie, but it's that critter I mentioned before, that attacked and made me reveal myself to my friends. It nearly hit you with this green fireball or something."

Bennie's scrapes seemed to hurt less when the nerves set in when she realized she was being attacked by a lot more than an interested guy. They both looked up over the trash cans, and ducked as more green fireballs slammed into the trashcans and sailed over their heads.

"Whatever it is it won't come out of the trees," Peter said. "So we don't have to worry about moving out into the open yet."

The trashcans were shuddering and Bennie had to set one right before it fell over again. She could tell by its weight that the other side was gone and the bag had slipped out.

"I think we do, actually," she groaned. "These plastic cans are no match for whatever shit that thing is hitting them with."

She and Peter both looked around. His house was still several yards away, and there was no other shelter until the trees behind their neighbor's house, which was a run straight in front of the trees across the road where the creature was.

"Any suggestions?" Peter said in a strained voice.

"Um, fight?" Bennie said. "It's better than waiting for them to finish the trashcans, and it could hold them off for a bit until we can figure out something better."

"I can't shoot diamond bullets into blind space," Peter said. "But fire away if you wish–no pun intended."

Bennie nodded and turned around. Only a bit of trash and plastic kept her safe. She had to time her appearance above the top of the cans between throws from the strange creatures.

Thud. The can shuddered again.

One...two...

Thud.

Two seconds.

"Bennie," Peter said as she counted. She missed her chance.

"What?" she snapped, a little harsher than she meant to.

"I was hoping to do this tactfully but since I may not get another chance at all…" Peter paused.

"Say it now," Bennie finished his thought and prepared for the next pause.

"Bennie, if we make it out of here alive, will you go out with me?" Peter said abruptly as the next fireball hit the last of the trash cans they hid behind.

This stopped Bennie short as she sprung up above the cans, head in view of their attacker. She was so shocked she forgot to cast her blow. She dropped down quickly as one of the green and flaming balls sailed in front of her nose, losing her balance.

"*Why* are you asking me this *now?*" she hissed, as he helped her right herself.

"It may be the only chance I get," he said, looking like he felt really stupid.

Well he is.

The next green ball began to melt Bennie's side of the trash can.

Now or never!

With lightning speed she popped up over the top of the can and fired lighting into the trees.

She was barely aware she had just managed the shotgun technique when another green, flaming ball struck her in the stomach.

"BENNIE!" Peter screamed, but Bennie couldn't speak or even scream in pain as the wind was knocked out of her. She was thrown back onto the ground, gasping as the acidic flames burned slowly into her.

Hissing, stinging itching burns as the acid ate away her skin…

That's bad, I think it'll kill me, Bennie managed to think, but was unable to find shock or fear as her senses started to dull.

Get up and help Peter you dolt…

But her body wouldn't move, frozen by the pain.

She looked up helplessly as Peter spun around to face the figure–no, *figures*–appearing in her quickly blurring sight. He formed a small, glittering knife with the small diamond he always had on him and jumped at them.

Got to press the A-1 keys, auto fight…

Bennie's mind was slipping…

No, no…not the game…Peter…

There was light…

"She's waking up."

"Bennie! Bennie? Can you hear me?"

Bennie thought for a moment it was her mom calling her, but with a voice strangely like a guy's.

Maybe the drugs for the wisdom teeth make you hear things funny…

"Yoo-hoo! Earth to Bennie!"

Another voice…

"Ben-jay! Shadow-chica! Hey, you're looking at me! Snap out of it!"

Wait…I'm not ready to get my wisdom teeth out…

"Give her a minute, she has to come around. I knew I shouldn't have let you all in!"

World of Warcraft–the guy looked like Peter…

PETER!

"Press the A-1 keys…" Bennie's tongue finally moved as she slowly began remembering things.

It was *Peter, not a game…*

"What is she talking about?" That was Gemini.

"Oh my God!" Sean was laughing.

"Peter, I swear if you've brainwashed her-"

"Perce!" Bennie realized she had been staring at him for a long time but hadn't registered it.

"About time you blinked, girl," Perce said softly, stroking her hair.

"Peter, where's Pete-I just heard him."

Peter came into view as Perce made room for him. He had blood on his shirt, but evidently Aila had already fixed him up because he had no visible injuries.

"Bennie? You scared the shit out of me!" He said.

Very gentlemanly.

"Fine! I'll go out with you! Don't distract me next time!" Bennie said, trying to sit up, and groaning as shooting aches seared through her abdomen. They were less than what she had felt earlier, but were still enough to leave her horizontal.

"What's all this?" Perce said, looking genuinely confused for the first time since Bennie had met him.

Aila was already speaking over him, telling Bennie she had to stay put for the potions to finish restoring the damaged tissue.

"No seriously, I want to know-" Perce was saying, and Bennie couldn't place the expression on his face.

"Pete! Did you really-"

"Shut up, Sean."

"Aila, what got her anyway?" Gemini was saying.

"Someone *please* tell me what Bennie just meant!"

"Perce-" Bennie began.

"Pete! Are you seriously saying you *asked* her out in the middle of a fight?"

"I didn't want to lose the chance!"

"What are you *talking about?*"

"Perce-"

"Was it a dragon?"

"I didn't mean to distract her-it just came out!"

"Peter!"

"What Perce?"

"I've heard of dragons spitting acid like that but how could he hide in the city?"

"Peter, you can't seriously think you can just ask Bennie-"

"Wait–Perce!" Bennie was getting totally lost in the noise, and for some reason, it made her want to cry.

"HEY!"

Everyone stopped and stared at Aila. The little fairy was puffed up, staring up at them sternly.

"Out, now, all of you!" she said, quieter now. "I won't have this chaos in my infirmary, and Bennie certainly doesn't need it! Out!"

There was no arguing. Tiny as she was, Aila could scold a grown man into silence. Bennie had seen it firsthand, and the feisty little fairy would have no nonsense on her ground. They all slid out quietly.

Perce was the last one out, looking regretfully at Bennie and eyeing Aila. He moved his mouth as if to say something a few times before finally closing it and shutting the door behind him.

Bennie blinked after him, contemplating how both times she had come to–after the lightning and now, he had been the first face she'd seen.

"You alright, sweetheart?" Aila said very gently, unlike her previous manner. "You're very lucky. That acid was slow acting or else it would have eaten away your internal organs before I got the anti-acid and restoratives on you."

"What exactly happened?" Bennie asked. "I remember Peter knife-fighting with someone–or something at least–and a bright flash before waking up here."

"That's more or less when the skirmish ended," Aila said, helping Bennie sit up. The pain had reduced to a steady stomachache but nothing more.

"When you got hurt Peter tried to fend them off to get you to safety," Aila went on, moving to a cabinet to put away the bottles and strange-looking first aid kit she had out. "The light you saw was probably the mage who came to help out. He said he caused a distraction so Peter had time to move you-and light works well on the eyes of many dark creatures. By all means it certainly wasn't any normal street gang that came after you, the claw slashes both Peter and your new friend had on them were unearthly-and poisoned to boot."

"What was the mage doing around Peter's house?" Bennie asked. "Peter said just the other day he doesn't know of any local Guardians, aside from himself…"

She trailed off as something occurred to her.

"…He wasn't… *following* us, was he?"

Aila turned and gave Bennie a curious look.

"Why would you need following?" Aila said evasively.

"That's what I'd like to know," Bennie said, staring unblinkingly at Aila for any hint.

"He may have just been visiting someone from out of town and gone for a walk," Aila said, turning back to the bottles she was reshelving. "I'd say ask him, but he took off to report the incident as soon as he was treated. Whatever his reasons, it was a good thing he was there when he was, or God knows what would have happened."

"We'd probably be dead," Bennie said, and added under her breath, "Or worse."

Aila's back stiffened momentarily, but she said nothing for the moment as she shut the cabinet doors.

"Well, you're fine for now," she finally said quietly. "Take it easy on the food for a while or you'll upset your stomach even more than it's probably annoying you now."

Chapter Twenty-One, Spies and Lies

Bennie found Perce, Sean, Gemini, and Peter all waiting quietly outside, the racket of questions, arguments, and teasing aptly silenced by Aila's formidable display.

Bennie, stressed, confused, and with the sickest stomach in her life, was not about to mince words with anyone. She wanted straight answers from Perce and Perce alone, but she didn't want anyone else around.

"Bennie-" Peter started.

"Just call me later- I'm still feeling icky, just want to lie down," Bennie said, putting on as calm a voice as she could. "Mind taking me home, Perce?"

"No problem," Perce said, his usual joking self.

He has no idea what trouble he's in, Bennie thought with some wicked amusement.

"I'll see y'all later," Bennie gave Sean and Gemini hugs.

"Be careful," Gemini said with force enough to make anyone believe she'd kill them with a look if they disobeyed.

* * *

"Perce, we need to talk," Bennie said once they were alone.

"Uh-oh, are you breaking up with me?" Perce said, pulling on a 'horrified' face.

"Perce, it's not funny." Bennie said irritably. "You've not told me something and I know it."

Perce was quiet as Bennie quickly ranted about how Aila had explained about the Guardian who just happened to be in the vicinity when she and Peter were attacked.

"Perce, I'm fifteen but I'm not a fool. The acid Reyortsed's goons attacked me with was too slow to kill me before help could arrive, that's what Aila said. And she wouldn't lie.

"And to top it off, the random mage was there to jump right in and take over, when Peter knows for a fact no other Guardians live within 20 miles of his house.

"Since there were only the two of us, really, why would Reyortsed have anyone there at all? Surely the area can't be that important to them, and if they were seeking out the mage they'd have looked for him in a more obvious place, wouldn't they? Because I highly doubt they'd be able to follow him without his knowing.

"There were at least five of those critters there, more than anyone with common sense would send one person to follow, so he wasn't following *them.*"

Perce never broke eye contact with her. He was taking her very seriously. Bennie was glad.

"The mage was following us wasn't he? Notice he didn't show himself until he knew we wouldn't win. He wouldn't want to blow his cover too easily."

Perce waited a moment to make sure she was finished before answering.

"Yes, he was following you." Perce said.

As much as she had believed it, Bennie still felt shocked to know that someone had been sneaking behind her every move.

"But why? And how long has he been following us? What *requires* that?"

Perce sighed.

"Sometimes Guardians are sent to keep an eye on people–some are spies and some are protectors. Like you said, he only showed himself when you needed him. That's why he was there, in case you needed help."

"Oh, so you're telling me *every* little, untrained Guardian has a stalker to keep them out of trouble? Are there really that many Guardians to spare that have nothing better to do but watch for jumps in the least likely places? *We* were in an unlikely place for an attack- which you still haven't explained, I haven't forgotten it. We're not anywhere near a danger zone and wow! We just happen to actually need that poor, bored guy who has to follow us.

"Perce, don't try to make me believe that because you know I won't."

Perce was quiet for a long time. Bennie wondered if he was even going to answer her, but he did.

"Bennie, you have to understand there are some things I am not at liberty to tell you, or anyone. You are right, not everyone has a 'bodyguard.' Only the people who need the protection badly need it.

"You have no idea how helpful your unknown friend has been. Do you remember when you were attacked back in the summer, when you lost your eyesight?"

"How can I forget?" Bennie said, pushing down the emotions that accompanied the unhappy memory. Her eyesight even flickered slightly before coming back.

"They would have had you if you had been alone. You couldn't see what you were doing. You had no idea *what* to do aside from become a human flamethrower-effective yes, but still poor odds against your enemies. We knew then we had to be sure your safety was ensured-"

"Why, because I can't take care of myself?" Bennie snapped.

"No! I didn't mean that," Perce said. "Bennie, I wish I could tell you what I mean but I just-"

"No, you can't tell me anything because *I* might get caught since I'm such a weakling, and Reyortsed obviously wants me alive instead of dead so I need to have plausible deniability when he finally gets me! Maybe I should just quit this whole business and forget everything that has happened to me!"

And with that Bennie stormed into the house and slammed the door, not giving Perce a chance to defend himself.

Chapter Twenty-Two, Keys

Bennie stayed home from practice and training the next day, truthfully feeling too sick to go anywhere. Out of common sense she told her mom it was something she ate, not a ball of slow-acting acid and a set of potions and anti-acids administered the previous afternoon and evening.

She got online later that evening to talk to her friends, and felt a pang when Sean sent her an instant message.

HadrianSF7: Chica, what happened?

Bennie ignored him and continued to talk to her other friends. Sean should know by now that they couldn't get any privacy on this screen name, which was why she created the other one.

He kept sending her instant messages, nevertheless, so she finally responded.

BenJ09: Sean, it's not a good time.

HadrianSF7: Better than some. Perce told me you were upset but he didn't tell me why. I was worried that you were hurt worse than we knew.

BenJ09: No, have a sick stomach but I'm not hurt badly.

<u>BenJ09:</u> I'm really not in the mood to talk about it right now, ok?

<u>HadrianSF7:</u> ok, but you know I'm around.

<u>BenJ09:</u> Ok.

Honestly, Bennie was curious as to why Perce had told Sean anything. He never really talked to her about Gemini or Sean, but then he probably didn't have people secretly following them.

So what makes me so weak and vulnerable? Bennie thought irately. *If I knew what it was...*

Bennie scratched an itch on her shoulder, and stopped. She pulled the sleeve back from her other shoulder and looked at the mark she'd found after being hit by the lightning.

It was still there, clear as ever. No sunshine had evened out her skin tone.

Perce has this tattooed on his finger. Maybe it's something dangerous to Reyortsed that he wants destroyed.

Or maybe, Bennie thought miserably, *Its dangerous to* us.

<u>BenJ09:</u> Sean?

<u>HadrianSF7:</u> Yo.

<u>BenJ09:</u> don't go anywhere.

<u>HadrianSF7:</u> :o

BenJ09 signed off at 9:06 pm.

Shadowchild7 signed on at 9:07 pm.

<u>HadrianSF7:</u> Must be important if you switched sn's.

<u>Shadowchild7:</u> I dunno, I just wanted to avoid all the extra IM's.

<u>HadrianSF7:</u> Zup?

<u>Shadowchild7:</u> Do you know what the tattoo on Perce's finger means, by any chance?

<u>HadrianSF7:</u> Do you?

<u>Shadowchild7:</u> No, I'd not be asking if I did.

HadrianSF7: I'm really not sure. I asked him before and he said a long time ago his best friend gave him that tattoo personally.

Shadowchild7: So it's just a silly "I woke up and didn't remember how I got it" thing?

HadrianSF7: That's what I assumed, but he wasn't very forthcoming with details.

HadrianSF7: Why?

Shadowchild7: I don't know, I was just curious.

HadrianSF7: Ben-jay, you didn't just get online to ask me about a *tattoo.*

Shadowchild7: No, I didn't.

HadrianSF7: So Talk :-P

Shadowchild7: Well, don't mention this to anyone-Perce already knows, but I have a mark from where the lightning hit me that looks exactly like that tattoo.

Shadowchild7: So I wanted to know if it had something to do with why I'm being followed by the mage who helped me and Peter.

HadrianSF7: Who-what?

Shadowchild7: Yeah, Perce didn't deny it. And since I can't find a reason why I'd need a bodyguard I figured it had something to do with this mark thing.

HadrianSF7: Did you ask him?

Shadowchild7: Like you said, he wasn't very forthcoming with details. I didn't figure out the mark thing until just now. I'd all but forgotten I had it.

HadrianSF7: Well, we missed you at practice. Perce said you were going through the "Maybe I shouldn't be doing this phase" and that you were pretty upset.

Shadowchild7: *phase?*

HadrianSF7: Yeah. Just about every Guardian has a moment or two when they think they'll just abandon their abilities. Only problem is when they try they find the powers tend to come back to haunt them. In other words, don't try just for the sake of time.

Shadowchild7: Huh. I'm surprised Perce didn't try telling me that. >:(

HadrianSF7: Well, no offense, but who listens when they're mad?

Shadowchild7: True.

HadrianSF7: You know he really does care about you. About all of us. He was so down tonight, and it's just not the same after all the months of you blasting things to pieces.

Shadowchild7: Are you trying to make me feel bad?

HadrianSF7: Yes. lol j/k

Shadowchild7: Well it's working.

Shadowchild7: I love you guys, you know. I get along better with Perce than I ever have with my mom.

HadrianSF7: Maybe it has something to do with the fact Perce actually knows you spend your nights fighting dark creatures and she doesn't?

Shadowchild7: My mom is not stupid. She knows, but she knows I won't listen because it's not something I can ignore-as you've established.

Shadowchild7: Perce is different because he actually *helps.*

HadrianSF7: Same for me. My dad is useless. Never paid child support, and left me and my mom with nothing. But Perce really in a way took his place.

Shadowchild7: Yeah. I never knew my dad. Perce did though.

HadrianSF7: He did?

Shadowchild7: According to my mom.

HadrianSF7: That's crazy!

Shadowchild7: Yeah. Maybe he got his tattoo from my dad.

HadrianSF7: Never know.

Shadowchild7: I guess I'll ask him sometime if he'll answer me.

HadrianSF7: Well you have to come to practice! I want to know now too!

Shadowchild7: Will do, when my stomach stops hurting. lol

After Bennie signed off a while later she thought about how Perce and her dad could possibly have known each other, and what link he may have had to the strange mark she and Perce shared.

Maybe that's why he died, and mom lied about the accident.

Based on everything that had happened in the past months, Bennie wouldn't have been surprised if that was the truth.

But no one will tell me, not yet anyway. I just hope it doesn't kill anyone else before I get the answers I need, or even after that.

Chapter Twenty-Three, Old Feuds

Bennie spent the next day going back and forth on whether or not she should go to Pelanca that night. Well, she knew she should, but if she could was her question.

I was such a jerk to Perce, she thought. Embarrassing to go and just show up like nothing happened.

But she wasn't ready to apologize either. Perce had to understand that she wanted answers and she wouldn't back down until she knew what was going on.

Bennie plunked on her bed and tried for the thirtieth time to read her summer reading, *Jane Eyre.*

So dull, so obvious, Bennie groaned as Rochester rambled on for pages to Jane about why he lied to her. *Oh wow-wee, he got sick of his first wife and instead of trying to talk to her about his peeves he locked her up as a "lunatic" and* voila! *She became one. He'd make a lunatic out of me, being all "woe is me!" like that. Idiot.*

Bennie blew exasperatedly through her lips and threw the book onto the floor. There was no way she was going to be able to finish the stupid thing in time for school. Two weeks away and she wasn't even to chapter thirty.

Grapes of Wrath, Bennie thought, *Now that's a good summer reading assignment. I should have read it last.*

Bennie looked at the clock and sighed.

8:39.

She had hoped to read so late into the night that she would "forget" practice and Perce.

Suddenly Bennie laughed.

Who can forget Perce? He's a nutcase without being an idiot. Mad or not, I'd rather spend the night around him and Sean and Gemini than Rochester!

Bennie crept out the back door after checking to make sure her mom was sleeping. No need for her to find out now.

But Bonnie was a better faker than her daughter knew, and she watched her daughter run away down the road towards the school.

"Damn you, Perce." Bonnie muttered, and sat to wait for her daughter to come home.

If she ever would.

Bennie was panting when she caught up with Sean at the school. Gemini and Perce were there too, which was curious. Neither Gemini nor Perce really lived in San Antonio, and they always met up with Sean and Bennie in Pelanca itself.

Oh god, I hope they weren't planning to come drag me out of my hole themselves. My mom would die.

But the "Bonnie and Bennie! Never apart!" taunts that flashed through Bennie's mind at that moment faded when she saw Gemini's face. Then Perce's and Sean's, which mirrored her expression.

"Hey Bennie," Sean said. "Good thing you showed up."

"I was hoping you would," Perce said, reaching out to pull Bennie into a one-armed hug, which she accepted. She suddenly realized how bad she felt about being mean to him.

"I have a feeling we're not practicing tonight, though," Bennie said, looking up into Perce's smile. But it was burdened and sad today, and it hurt Bennie somewhere inside when she looked at it.

"No, we're not," He said, gathering Gemini in his other arm.

Gemini was even worse to look at. She had always been radiant, sometimes literally. Now she looked limp and dim as a dead pixie. She just leaned into Perce's embrace, resting her head on his shoulder. When Sean tried to give her a comforting pat on the shoulder, she turned away from him. Sean bit his lip.

"I need to talk to you, Bennie," Perce said, "Gemini's in a tight spot right now."

"What happened?"

"Dwendol fell," Gemini said, her voice strained and sharp. None of the wily grace she used in her skills was there now.

Bennie just stared. An entire planet, one of the most powerful at that, completely overrun by Reyortsed?

"You're not serious."

Perce closed his eyes and held Gemini closer.

"We couldn't spare the Guardians in Pelanca. We had to let it happen."

"Sick," Sean hissed, but Perce said nothing. They all knew it was a sacrifice that had to be made, they just hadn't expected it so soon.

Gemini's eyes opened, startling Bennie as they blazed with a genuine glow of pure rage.

"My family is still there," She said. "I was off, gallivanting around in Pelanca. I should have been there. Reyortsed's men would never have known what hit them."

Her eyes faded again, and she looked like she believed she'd have been useless after all.

Perce cradled her in his arms. Bennie remembered when he'd taken care of her after she had panicked when she lost her eyesight.

He's all the family she has now, Bennie thought, *me and Sean too.*

"Like I said, Gemini is in a tight spot," Perce said. "She can't very well go home at the present time, and Sean and I can't take her in, being guys and all. It'd be awkward."

Bennie realized what Perce was saying.

"If she needs to stay with me I say yes, here and now, but convincing my mom-"

"Is the problem, I know." Perce said, "You never told her about us and all this, did you?"

Bennie shifted. "*My* mom? She'd lock me up, either to protect me or because she'd think I was insane."

"Not without reason, the protection part I mean," Perce said bitterly.

Bennie looked up at him sharply, but Perce shut his mouth without divulging anything more.

"We'll see to it, together," was all he finally said.

Bennie led the other three to her home and stopped short.

"What's up, Ben-jay?" Sean said.

Bennie barely registered his voice before shouting, "Double shit!" and running towards the brightly lit house.

Her mom was waiting for her, all the lights on, on the couch.

"That didn't take long, Benjamina," She said, arms folded.

Sean caught up behind her and stood in the doorway, not entirely sure what to do next.

"Oh? And who's your friend? I'll admit I was expecting you to be with-"

She paused as her initial assumptions were confirmed when Perce appeared. Gemini held back.

"Ah, yes, *you* of course," Bonnie rose from the sofa, eyeing Perce. "Come to take my daughter off with your secret society too? I *won't* have it, Perce."

Perce stepped forward, his features strange in Bennie's eyes. This expression was unlike anything she had ever seen.

"You know better than that, Bonnie," he said quietly.

"Oh I *do* know better! Better than to let you drag off all I have left in the world!"

Bennie flinched as her mom jerked her back suddenly. "What you do is your call, but my daughter won't be forced into anything! I don't know what curse she's got but she doesn't need you around making it a bigger deal than it is! She can get along without it."

"Bonnie!" Perce said sharply. "You *know* no one is forced into this, and you know she's more of a threat without training!"

"I don't give a fuck about it!" Bennie flinched when her mom swore. It was so painful to hear her say what Bennie only expected from a stupid high school student, not a grown woman. "You teaching her how to control whatever you did to her will lead to silly notions about protecting the world from the devil and God-knows-what, and that's exactly what led to my husband getting killed in that--accident!"

Bennie caught the pause, but her mom never looked her way.

Perce's grey eyes grew dark and distant.

"One, I didn't do anything to your daughter. She was chosen for the *gifts* she got, just as Caleb was. Two, I wouldn't let anything happen to Bennie, not as along as I'm alive. I owe Caleb that much, and you and Bennie so much more.

"And thirdly, you need to realize you can't lie to yourself or to Bennie anymore. There was no *accident.* It may be easier to believe, but there wasn't. I know. *I was there.*"

Bennie, Sean and Gemini had all been watching this scene unfold in complete silence. But now Sean and Bennie both gasped slightly, and Gemini even looked up with some of her old awareness about her, eyes on the two now facing off.

"Lies, all of it!" Bonnie snapped, gripping Bennie's now purple arm even harder. "If Caleb hadn't been goofing off with you he wouldn't have gotten into trouble. He never asked for any of this, nor did Bennie, nor I!"

Perce looked at her sadly.

"None of us asked for this," he said quietly.

"But none of us rejected it, either." Bennie interjected, pulling her arm from her mother's grasp. "Including me."

She stepped away from the group.

"Now I don't know what the hell happened between you and Perce, mom," Bennie snarled. "He's as open and honest about the past as you!"

Perce looked down when she said this, but Bennie's mom just looked at her with utter shock, as if Bennie had hit her.

"But I know about here and now, and that is this: One, I have some really freaky abilities that I don't dare risk losing control of at school. Two, my friend Gemini's home planet is now in the grasp of some maniac and she can't go back, and so she's staying with me!"

Bennie walked over and took Gemini's hand.

"And thirdly, since I want to keep from blowing something up by accident, and since I want Gemini to get home sooner than later, and since you obviously let my dad be who he was once upon a time, I'm going to keep being who I am, and that is Shadowchild!"

Bennie was shouting by now, fire flowing through her veins, electricity through every nerve in her body. She vaguely imagined sending a spark into the lamp beside her to dim the room and show her mom how she dissolved in darkness, but she didn't trust the charge to be small enough not to cause serious damage.

Hands hot, she let go of Gemini as sparks ran on her fingers. Gemini was dead silent. Everyone was silent.

For a long moment they just stood there, Bennie panting as the electricity slowly died down on her hands, Sean still backed against the doorway, Gemini standing alone, and Perce and Bonnie staring at Bennie now.

Bonnie blinked first, tears in her eyes.

"My Benjamina," she said, "What have they done to you?"

Something in her mother's voice unsettled Bennie.

This was not the fierce and stubborn lawyer she knew her mom to be. This wasn't the paranoid prefix tied to her name in the days of third grade teasing. This was someone very small, very lost, and very, very scared.

"Mom?"

Bonnie spun around, fled to her room, and slammed the door in Bennie's face.

"Mom!"

Bennie tried the door, but it was locked. She looked at Perce.

"Unlock the door! Talk to her–do *something!*"

Perce was staring at the door.

"What did *they* do to *you,* Bonnie?" he said, so quietly Bennie thought she had heard his thoughts.

"Perce?"

He looked away and shook his head.

"It was a mistake," he said.

"What?"

"Everything," Perce said, "Leaving her alone all these years, trying to be your teacher, bringing us all here. I should have known better."

"Perce!"

"No, Bennie, I won't unlock the door."

"Perce, what the hell is going on?"

Perce looked up and Bennie was shocked to see his eyes swimming.

"I'll tell you what's going on. I'm leaving now. I'm only making things worse."

Bennie stared at him.

"What? N-no! You can't just leave me here with her!"

"I can't do anything, Bennie."

"You set her off! That's sure as hell doing something!"

"No, I set her *up. You* set her off."

"I did not!"

"Bennie, it wasn't until you sided with me that she broke down. You saw. She was her feisty, stubborn self up until that point."

"She's never been like–*that*." Bennie was still spooked by her mother's sudden change.

"Exactly. The Bonnie I knew sixteen years ago had no vulnerabilities. This Bonnie is scared, hurt, and not without reason.

"I thought then that maybe it was wise to leave her alone like she asked when your dad died. Now I see I'm wrong. She's believed in lies too long, and that's my fault for not being there."

Bennie remembered something.

"But you were there, when my dad died."

Perce was quiet.

"You said yourself you were there, and that it wasn't an accident!" Bennie said, growing loud again. "Perce! I trust you, but how can I anymore if you won't tell me what really happened? How do you know my parents? Why is my dad dead? What is my mom scared of? And what do I have to do with any of it? Why won't you tell me?"

Perce was holding his head as he shook it, as if something wanted to get out.

"I'm sorry. I need time to think."

"Think? I think I can't do anything until I know the truth."

"Yes! Yes, perfect, don't do anything." Perce said, looking at her clearly.

"That wasn't what I expected…" Bennie said.

"Don't do anything," Perce said. "I'm going to find somewhere else for Gemini to stay, and leave you and Bonnie alone for a bit."

Bennie fumed.

"I *told* you, you can't leave me with her! Not now! I need you!"

Tears streamed down her face now, but she didn't care.

"Up until a few months ago I was just getting on with life and then you came along! If the lightning had hit me and I'd not had someone there to point out my changes *I'd* have locked myself up and submitted to dissection and research. But no, you were there! And when that-that *demon* showed up you took care of me! And you came back after the fight. I knew you wouldn't ever leave me all alone again after that! And now you're just going to walk off after screwing things over with my mom and me? Just like that? I can't believe you! When I need you most you just run off and don't come back!"

Perce reached out and put his hands on her trembling shoulders.

"Leave *you?* Did I ever say I was leaving *you?*"

Bennie blinked at him. "You just did, stupid."

Perce smiled ruefully.

"I didn't mean leaving you. I meant I was leaving right now before your mom comes out with a butcher knife and starts attacking us. I need time to think about how we're going to settle this, and help your mom, because she's going to need it, having as special a daughter as she does.

"I'd never leave you, Bennie. I never left your dad, I shouldn't have left your mom, and I won't leave you. I'm going to tell you everything; I just need to know where to start."

He sat her down on the sofa, kneeling in front of her to look her in the eyes.

"You need to know, and you will, I promise you that, but right now we all need to calm down, clear out, and let your mom get ahold of the world. I was stupid to come barging in here expecting her to see reason. What can I say? I've not been alone with my fears for sixteen years and I sure as hell am no shrink so I don't know what to do."

Bennie smiled weakly. That was obvious.

"So yes, don't do anything, no magic tricks, no fighting, no calling yourself Shadowchild in front of your mom. Just be good to her, even when she's being a nut, and I'll be back to settle things once and for all.

"And as for Sean and his pals, I doubt they'll leave you to put up with any trouble alone."

Perce leaned forward to hug Bennie, and she fell into his arms.

"I'll be back," Perce said, "But I want this same Bennie to be here, all fingers and toes. Promise to be careful and remember what we've learned."

"Promise," Bennie mumbled into his coat.

Perce held her for a moment longer before letting go.

"Gem and I will try Jinx's and see if she's got space. Call Sean if anything comes up and he'll get it to me stat."

Sean nodded. He'd be close by no matter what.

With some quiet, if not quick, goodbyes Gemini and Perce disappeared into the night. Sean lingered for a moment to make sure Bennie was going to be ok.

When he was gone, Bennie went into the garage and found a screwdriver.

I'll just do what she does when she needs to get into a locked room, Bennie thought grimly as she removed the entire door knob to her mom's bedroom.

Bonnie was curled in a fetal position on top of the blankets on the bed. She was very much asleep this time, and Bennie, fearful to touch her face, rested her hand on the pillow.

Damp.

Bennie tiptoed up to her room and pulled a blanket off her bed. Grabbing her pillow and her old stuffed bunny, Lucky, she crept into her mom's room and crawled into the bed.

I haven't done this since I had that nightmare in the second grade about the black frog eating up the house. Bennie thought.

She carefully pulled a blanket over her mom, and one over herself. She curled up and watched her mom's back rise and fall with her quiet breathing.

Bennie laced her fingers in her mom's shoulder-length blonde hair. It was so soft.

Mommy... Bennie felt a pang of guilt, and watched her mom through her tears for a very long time.

But even Guardians sleep, and when Bennie awoke in the morning, she was alone in the bed, with Lucky.

Her mom said nothing of the night before.

Chapter Twenty-Four, Patience

Bennie still had no word from Perce over two weeks later, shortly after she started the tenth grade at Marshall.

She walked the hallways in silence, marveling at how much had changed since her first day here last year, and not just the fact that she knew her way around the halls.

Last year I didn't know Perce, she thought. *I wasn't waiting on him. I could focus on normal stuff, like filling out the endless stream of information sheets these teachers love to hand out.*

But now Bennie could hardly think straight. She was tired, even though as a Guardian she needed nearly no sleep. She kept forgetting her homework assignments, repeatedly turning them in for late grades. Her mom never said anything if she knew about Bennie's problems; she said nothing at all. The silence was torture.

If she'd just talk to me! She doesn't even ask me where I'm going when I go see my friends in the afternoon.

Bennie buried her face in her hands and slumped forward on her desk. The geometry was giving her a headache.

Maybe she doesn't care anymore. Maybe she hopes I'll just go away...

Bennie was startled by a tapping on her shoulder.

"Miss James?" Mr. Franks said formally, "That was the bell."

"Oh? I didn't hear it, thanks."

Bennie started shoving her stuff into her bag when she noticed Mr. Franks was still looking at her.

"You don't look like you're feeling well," was all he said. But like some teachers, there was a deeper perception layered under the words.

But Bennie didn't want to talk.

"I'm fine, just tired," She said, "Not used to getting up early again yet."

"I see." But the blue eyes never blinked as she hurried out of the room to lunch.

Later on Bennie pondered over the geometry assignment she had copied off the board before drifting off. Having no luck she stopped by Sean's house for a little tutoring, and to see if Perce had contacted him at all.

Sean said he hadn't heard anything either and that he was actually meeting with Perce's friend Marek to work on his flying skills.

"No shape shifting work for the moment," he said as he fought with some random creature on his WOW game. Peter's voice came over the online speaker, making fun of him for losing the fight and becoming a wisp.

"What about Gemini?" Bennie said, sighing as she finally completed the assignment. "Thanks for the old geometry notes, by the way."

"Figured they'd come in handy for something, although keeping notebooks from every year of high school tends to build up," he remarked, looking into his war zone of a closet, then proceeded to reclaim his body on the computer screen. "As for Gemini, she's still staying with Jinx's family. Speaking of family, has your mom said anything to you?"

"No," Bennie muttered, thinking about the uncomfortable silence that had settled in her house. "If she ever speaks to me again it'll be a miracle."

"She'll come around," Peter said, surprising Bennie that he could hear her. "From what you told me she had to know you were doing something, if not fighting."

"I just hope she comes around sooner rather than later," Bennie remarked. "I'm used to her never shutting up and leaving me alone, but now she won't even look me in the eye. It's been nearly three weeks!"

"Well, you can always try talking to her yourself, instead of waiting."

"Already did," Bennie said. "She just said she was kind of busy and could I leave her alone for a bit."

"Never hurts to keep trying," Sean remarked, adding more loot to his store from a recent kill.

"Hmm," Bennie said, but she was really thinking: *If she was ever home these days, I'd try again.*

Chapter Twenty-Five, Evacuation

Bennie was reading when she heard a tapping on her window. She lifted one of the blinds slightly and peered out through the darkness. She jumped in surprise when she saw Sean lean down over the roof's edge and look at her. She opened the window.

"Sean?" Bennie said. "What's up? It's 3:30 in the morning; you know what my mom would think!"

"It doesn't matter now, we've got bigger problems," Sean said. "Perce ran off."

"What? Where?" Bennie said, leaning dangerously out of the window.

"I'll explain in a minute. Get dressed while I shift and I'll fly us out of here without bugging your mom."

Bennie did as she was told, pulling on her special-made clothes rapidly as possible as her fingers fumbled and her heart pounded with worry. Before long, she was flying on Sean's back, praying he had not left any over-large talon marks on the roof of the house.

Bennie forgot all about any damage Sean may have done to the house when they arrived in Pelanca. Aila's face was white with fury-and fear.

"Esla sent troops to Dwendol to help fight off Reyortsed's hold on the planet so the civilians could evacuate safely," She said. "Perce went with them. The fool! He has other responsibilities now! How many times do I have to tell him!"

"But it can't be that bad," Bennie said, not knowing why she did, especially after Gemini looked at her. The sadness in her eyes was like a sharp metal spike digging its way into Bennie's chest.

"He wouldn't go if he thought it was too dangerous. He'll be back!" Bennie spoke again as Gemini turned away.

"We don't know that, Bennie," Sean said. "Dwendol was one of the strongest, best fortified planets in the known universe, second only to Pelanca itself. If Reyortsed could take it down so quickly, he's a bigger threat than we ever knew."

"Then *why* did Esla send anyone there in the first place, if we had no chance of taking it back?" Bennie snarled.

"We're not taking it back, Bennie," Aila said, "We're abandoning it. The mission was soley to retrieve as many people as we could."

"My family is still there," Gemini said. "When Perce told me he would do all he could to help them, I had no idea he meant this. It's practically suicide!"

"He wouldn't have *gone* if he thought that!" Bennie said, getting all the more irritated at the others for acting like there was nothing they could do. She was more irritated with herself for not coming up with anything.

Aila just shook her head.

"He would," she said. "He always has something to prove. He wasn't always so reckless. Losing Allison hurt him more than he knew. Now he can't let anyone down."

"He wouldn't have let me down if he'd stayed!" Gemini said, her voice quivering. "We need him *here.*"

"Perce isn't that stupid--Allison?" Bennie didn't know the name, but it filled her with dread.

Sean and Aila just looked at each other. They were silent.

"*Who's --Allison?*" Bennie said, reminding them that she was still out of the loop.

"Perce's wife," Gemini said.

Bennie just looked at her, dumbstruck.

"Perce is *married?*" She said. "And this is the first I've heard of it? After all these months?"

"It never came up, I guess," Sean said. "She died years ago, and he thinks it's his fault."

Bennie just shook her head. This was too much.

"So Perce has something to prove to himself, and he forgets all about us in the process. So what do we do now?"

More silence.

"*Well?*"

"We wait, Bennie," Sean said. "That's all we can do."

Bennie stayed in Pelanca a few hours more, wanting to get answers from Aila about Perce and the life he'd once had. But the questions died in her throat when she saw how badly Aila was taking Perce's disappearance. She seemed to know him better than anyone else. She'd most certainly known him the longest.

At about 5 in the morning she decided she'd best get home before her mom woke up and saw she was gone.

"Let me know as soon as word comes about Perce, even if I'm in school," she remarked as she and Sean took the caves home.

Chapter Twenty-Six, Gone

Bennie was never happier to hear the final bell at school ring than the next few days. She knew she'd failed the algebra quiz she'd taken three days after Perce had vanished with the rescue teams into who-knows-what. She hadn't been able to focus at all. Math wasn't usually hard for her, but it wasn't something she could just throw off. She tried to push it out of her mind as she got on the noisy school bus, earphones playing as loud as possible over her screaming bus mates. It would have been quicker to walk and avoid the roundabout route, but Bennie wanted to take time to think.

As the bus hit bump after bump, as the kids trickled off at each stop and a little more fresh air made its way into the stuffy, sweltering bus, Bennie's mind wandered from the music and diminishing din to other things. Perce hadn't been able to get her back into training with him yet, he hadn't explained anything. She had so many questions, and the thought of never getting them answered-

No. He would answer them. She would see him again. Everything was going to be fine, he and the rest of the Guardians in Dwendol were just being quiet and careful about the evacuations.

The bus stopped at her street. Bennie pulled herself up off the vinyl seat, her skin sticking to it slightly and making a funny whoosh sound as she pulled away. Muttering thanks to the bus driver she started off down the road to her house, nodding goodbye to the other kids who had gotten off with her.

She slowed when she saw Sean standing by her mailbox. She searched his face for any sign of good news, but he looked grim as ever.

"The rescue teams came back to Pelanca today," Sean said before she could speak. "Gemini's family is safe, if worn out. It was a mess there, but I don't mean that everything was in ruins. There wasn't any damage to the capital at all."

"What happened?"

"Well, it's hard to say. Reyortsed apparently used some sort of hypnotic power on a great deal of the population. Nearly none of them wanted to leave. Those who did started moving to the tunnels as soon as they heard they had a chance to escape. But word about the Guardians was spreading. They were attacked when they went back for the last few families."

"What about Perce?" Bennie said, trying not to show her impatience.

Sean was very pale.

"His friend Marek got captured in the fight. Perce went after him."

"And?"

"Marek reappeared some hours later more or less unharmed. Said the guards were almost too easy to handle. But he hadn't come across Perce."

Bennie felt an odd spike in her chest. She struggled to breathe.

"When did Perce get back?" She whispered. She already knew the answer.

Sean's eyes were swimming, but no tears fell.

"He didn't come back, Bennie. Perce didn't come back at all."

Chapter Twenty-Seven, Another Chance

Bennie only went to school at all the next two days because the thought of being home alone drove her nuts. She stayed on the computer all night, aimlessly surfing the internet and finding no answers to the turmoil going on inside her.

She was on AIM, but Sean hadn't sent her a message, and she hadn't sent him one. They just sat apart in cyberspace, not sure what to say.

Bennie sighed, placing her head on the desk. She was so tired, but even if she had needed sleep, she couldn't have found it with a sedative or a knock on the head.

Her computer made a bloop-bleep sound. She looked up to find a message request on her screen:

"What?" Bennie said. Tentatively, she pressed the "Yes" button.

<u>i have him:</u> I assume you want your mentor back by now.

Bennie stared at the message; the spike in her chest was replaced by a throbbing, painful fear.

<u>Shadowchild7:</u> Who are you? How did you get my screen name?

<u>i have him:</u> I have my ways of finding things out very easily, and I think you know perfectly well who I am. And I know who you are, Benjamina James.

Bennie stared at the computer as if it had spoken to her itself. Reyortsed? On AIM? It was almost funny.

<u>i have him:</u> Now before you start asking me a bunch of stupid, redundant questions let me answer them: Yes, I have Perseus in my custody, and Guardians, such as he is, are prone to some unpleasant interrogations and eventually execution but since I can see you won't want that and I prefer not to kill people, I'm offering you a chance to save him.

Bennie's hands shook as she typed.

<u>Shadowchild7:</u> Why should I trust you?

<u>i have him:</u> Let me speak and I'll tell you why. You've noticed something about yourself, have you not? A strange mark, perhaps, on your shoulder?

Bennie held back a surge of panic. How did he know that?

<u>i have him:</u> You see, Shadowchild, that mark means something to me. It means you have something I desire more than anything else in the universe. It means little to you, if anything, and it'd be such a trifle for you to give to me, especially in exchange for Perce–as you call him.

Bennie knew he was manipulating her, but she felt something odd in herself. She really didn't care. What Reyortsed was saying made so much sense. She didn't even know what the mark meant, and if it was simply some sort of magical ability she couldn't even use, why did she need it? Perce was certainly worth more than that!

Bennie started shaking her head. No, he was doing something to her. He was trying to trap her...

<u>i have him:</u> Believe me, *Bennie*, you could never live with yourself if you knew you had the chance to save him, and instead left him alone to suffer and die at the hands of my officers. They're not as squeamish as I about that sort of thing.

Bennie was struggling hard to gain control of her senses, but the only sense she could find was what Reyortsed was saying. She started typing, defiance in the words she wrote and in her thoughts.

<u>Shadowchild7:</u> I don't believe you. Nor do I trust you.

<u>i have him:</u> Why *not*, Bennie?

Bennie was quiet, still, watching the following messages come through.

<u>i have him:</u> If you accept my offer meet me at your school tomorrow at midnight, in the courtyard where you sent all of San Antonio into a blackout. Come alone, tell no one. I'll be waiting.

i have him signed off at 2:34 am.

Bennie didn't move again until she heard her mom get up downstairs for work.

Chapter Twenty-Eight, Mind or Heart

11:00 pm, Saturday Night.

Bennie looked at herself in the mirror. She had dressed in the dark grey camisole, black pants, boots and long coat she had bought in Pelanca. They had been appealing to her not only because they could vanish with her invisibility easily, or because they were fireproof, but because they made her feel like one with the darkness, like Shadowchild.

She lifted her long hair and fastened the moonstone necklace Aila had given her around her neck. She was ready.

11:40 pm, Saturday Night

This is foolish, Bennie thought to herself. *You're not even through training yet. How are you supposed to beat someone if Reyortsed's just trying to trap you? Remember the lessons with Perce? "Don't accept a negotiation proposal that requires you to go somewhere alone and unarmed"?*

Another voice argued with her, a musical, mystical whisper:

What makes you important enough for Reyortsed to kill? He only wants the power you don't even know about, and you'll never finish training.

Bennie had finished lumping up the blankets in her bed. Mom would see a sleeping girl if she came upstairs at all, if she still even tried to assure herself Bennie was here.

With mixed feelings, Bennie slipped out the door and headed to the school.

12:00 am, Sunday—

Chapter Twenty-Nine, Reyortsed

Bennie lurked invisible in the shadows, looking for any sign of Reyortsed or his monsters hiding in it with her. She saw nothing hidden.

Either he's late, he lied, or he's hidden so well I'll only see him when I'm not hidden myself.

Bennie seriously contemplated leaving, but she couldn't. With every hard beat of her heart she heard "Perce, Perce, Perce."

Bennie stepped into the light, dead center in the courtyard.

"REYORTSED!" She shouted, sounding a lot braver than she felt. After the initial echo, all was quiet.

He lied. He's not here.

Bennie felt her breath heavy. It was the only sound-and then-

"Shadowchild…"

A whisper, a beautiful, beautiful whisper. Bennie instinctively tried to turn towards the sound, but it was everywhere.

"Shadowchild…"

Suddenly, Bennie saw movement in the darkness. A figure. Forming from thin air.

"Shadowchild..."

It was completely shaded from her view, but it was coming to the light.

"Shadowchild..."

Reyortsed stepped into the light. The echo ceased, but the sight was enough to fill the silence.

Bennie stared for what seemed like a very long time. Not only was his voice enrapturing-yes, there was no doubt he'd been speaking her name-his very presence was almost more than she could take.

He was inhuman. No man had such a flawless face, a face of strong yet soft angles, a pale olive color, a powerful nose that curved just so slightly, so gracefully, his lips, his perfect lips, were parted just so, Bennie wanted to touch her own to them. The long black hair framed that glorious face and draped over his shoulders, down his slender frame. The silvery black robes he wore showed that despite the graceful narrowness of his body, he was well muscled.

Not like a vampire...like an angel...a dark angel...

The shadow his hair cast on his face was lifted, and Bennie saw his eyes as he looked deeper into her. Black as the abyss, entirely black.

*Inhuman...*Bennie's reverie snapped. *Inhuman!* He was nothing like a human being anymore, whether he once was or not. He cared for nothing and no one. She stepped back.

But he was quicker. Those perfect lips opened again.

"Good evening, *Shadowchild.*"

His long finger traced her face. She felt herself sinking back under his control.

No...

She pried her eyes away from his, and moved away from his hand. She could still feel his touch on her skin, as hot as the fire and as cold as the lightning she threw.

"I...believe we had an arrangement." She said stubbornly.

"I believe we did," Reyortsed said, every syllable an unearthly note. Behind him two men appeared. They were hauntingly beautiful themselves, but nothing compared to Reyortsed. Bennie could see they were Dark Elves, and she saw even better the man they clutched between them.

Perce.

Bennie's heart began beating again. Perce, Perce, Perce.

Aside from a line of blood running down the side of his face, Perce looked unharmed, but the defiance in his face turned to horror when he saw Bennie.

Any spell of Reyortsed's that still remained on Bennie lifted then. And she realized she had made a deadly error.

"Now, Shadowchild, you see I have kept my side of the bargain, what about yours?"

Bennie really wasn't sure what to do now. She didn't even really know why she was here.

Stupid, stupid stupid!

"You can take what you want," Bennie said, trying to sound firm, "When I see Perce released."

"Very well, but can you convince *him* of that?" Reyortsed gestured smoothly towards Perce. "He's the one who has what I need."

Bennie felt a prickle of anger. This was not going right.

"Then what am I here for?" She said. She didn't dare look Reyortsed in the face again lest he gain control of her again.

"Because he can't give it to me, only you can," Reyortsed was saying. He bent down slightly to look Bennie in the eyes himself, and she braced herself. But the spell didn't come. Only the words, the voice...

"Benjamina, your father had a special gift, a gift I learned I was supposed to receive, but never did. It was stolen from me, and before your father died, he gave it to Perseus for safekeeping. Perseus cannot use it, only possess it, but you *can* use it. Perseus can give it only to you, but you can give it to anyone. All I ask is that you give it to me."

Bennie felt her mind drifting away on that voice just as she realized Perce's tattoo and the mark on her shoulder both meant they had this power, but that voice...

"Bennie," that was Perce. It was all he said, but Bennie awoke again. One of the elves clapped a firm hand over Perce's mouth. Bennie glared at the elf.

"Why should I give it to you?" She said, staring at Reyortsed now. He couldn't control her anymore.

"Because if you don't, I'll be forced to kill you, and Perseus," Even his sinister smile was seductive. "And you know how I *hate* to kill needlessly. It's not a reputable habit. But I will, because you are too dangerous to live if you have it, and I won't let him give it to you unless I know I can *trust you.*"

For Bennie, time seemed to stop for a moment.

She locked eyes with Perce.

This is why I was being followed all the time, this is why my mark isn't normal and you share it, this is why my dad is dead. This is why you left me alone, you kept your secrets, tried to protect me. And this is why we are here now, and I'm a fool.

Bennie knew Perce knew what she was thinking, and she knew he knew what she planned to do.

But then his eyes looked past her at something. Bennie felt cold suddenly.

"I can't let you leave unless I know for sure, Shadowchild, that you are no longer a threat to me and all I try to obtain. So I brought along a friend of mine, and I believe you know him."

Bennie tried not to turn, but she did as if someone pushed her.

The blackness cloaking Gregk the demon had no effect on her eyes as she looked upon him again.

He was alive after all. She hadn't killed anyone yet.

"Ah, she remembers my face," the demon said scathingly as Bennie's eyes began to mist over with black and she felt utter terror seize her soul. But she remembered the words Perce had spoken to her, the words Alia told her as she gave her the moonstone necklace: even on the darkest nights...

Bennie gripped the stone in her hand. She turned her eyes to the moon. There it was. Her heartbeat calmed for the first time that night.

She looked down at Gregk, and looked, and looked. He blinked in surprise when he realized she hadn't gone blind again.

"I do remember your face," Bennie hissed, "And I'm sad I didn't manage to mangle it more the first time I did this!"

Bennie drew up her hands and threw an enormous fireball straight at the demon, spiking it with bolts of lighting so strong the light bulbs in every lamp in the courtyard exploded, as did Gregk.

Gain experience in the World of Warcraft, kill to stay alive. It all makes sense now, if not much.

Faster than light Bennie had spun around and struck the elves in the chest with lightning. After the major surge she had struck Gregk with she was too drained to do anymore than stun them, but it gave Perce the slack he needed.

"Bennie!" He shouted, and sent a strong white spark from his hand. It hit her in the chest.

Bennie paused as she absorbed the shock of the power transfer, but as she did she understood Perce hadn't really sent her the power Reyortsed wanted. He'd merely sent her some more energy.

Reyortsed, who had apparently been slightly surprised that Gregk's presence had failed to incapacitate Bennie, immediately turned on Bennie as she continued absorbing the new strength.

"You have no fear of demons, girl," He said, not sounding quite so beautiful now, "But by destroying one, your power is drained, you cannot fight now."

Bennie panted, her whole body on pins and needles.

He thinks Perce sent me the power he wants, not an energy boost.

Energy...wait!

Bennie looked over at Perce as horror struck her.

He had fallen to his knees, white-faced.

Energy...his energy. He's defenseless!

One of the elves had come around again and dragged Perce to his feet like a rag doll. The other elf, on his feet again now too, muttered something and sent a dark red spark into Perce. The elves dropped him.

"Leave us," Reyortsed said. The confused elves did as they were told, and Bennie began to understand why Reyortsed was getting them away from her, what the power he thought she now had was.

But there were more pressing things at hand. Reyortsed demanded all of her attention once more.

"That incantation my elfin friend spoke will kill Perseus in minutes, Shadowchild," he said. "I know the spell to save him, but you know what I ask for first."

Bennie's heart was breaking. She looked at Perce again. He smiled at her. Their plan would work.

Bennie looked back at Reyortsed, her voice stronger than she felt.

"This power suits me, I'm afraid." she said, spinning a web of electricity and fire between her hands. "And I can see now that your power is of the same nature, so maybe I'll just take yours instead."

Bennie turned to fight Reyortsed, but saw only a dissolving form. He was leaving as quickly as his elves did.

And I still don't even really know why...

Bennie felt a moment of relief before she heard Perce.

"Bennie," he said, his voice faint.

Bennie turned around again. Perce was stretched out over the ground now.

Her heart stopped.

That incantation my elfin friend spoke will kill Perseus in minutes...

"Perce?"

"Come here, Bennie, quickly."

Bennie rushed over, lifting Perce's head into her lap.

"No, it was a bluff-it wasn't-"

"It doesn't matter, Bennie," Perce said, quieter than ever now. But his eyes were clear and focused on Bennie.

"No, Perce--"

"Bennie, there's not time for that, you have to promise me you'll get to Aila right away, nowhere else."

"Perce!"

"Give me your hand, sweetheart. Time will tell the rest."

Bennie felt tears in her eyes, and she wanted Perce to stop, but she couldn't deny it either. Perce was dying.

"Your hand, Bennie."

Bennie put her hand in his, and locked her eyes on his.

Please, take the extra energy back. It'll make you strong enough to fight the spell until we can get help...

But Perce wasn't taking anything from her. Bennie's hand grew hot. Their hands began to glow so brightly Bennie had to shut her eyes...

Faces, all with the same, deep grey eyes. Something red, flaming...erupted from inside her. Bennie looked down but all she saw of her body was fire...a sudden tingling in her flaming form...

And then a face she'd seen before...but never in person...

Dad.

Bennies eyes snapped open. Perce was still beside her, but this time, he was on the ground, and he did not wake up and see her smile.

Suddenly a burning in Bennie's heart grew very strong. Flames licked out of her skin, all over, not just her hands. Her tears evaporated in her eyes as she burst into flame.

Bennie screamed with agony from her heart. She felt no pain from the flames. They turned into scarlet and golden feathers. Her arms were wings. She felt herself transform as she screamed, and the scream transformed.

Phoenix Song.

Bennie rocketed into the air, a pillar of fire in her wake. Perce's body lay untouched down below, but she could not go to him.

Aila, go to Aila. He said go...

Bennie flew.

Chapter Thirty, Phoenix

Aila heard the call. No one had to tell her what it was even though nearly no one still alive had ever actually heard the sound.

She looked up and saw the phoenix coming down, the feathers turning into flames once more, the body transforming into a girl dressed in grey...

Benjamina.

Aila had no time to ponder what she saw. Bennie collapsed, nearly knocking the tiny fairy flat, tears still in her eyes.

Aila took Bennie inside. She knew what had happened.

Bennie did not remember much of when she got to Aila's. She only remembered a pure, uncontrollable need to sleep, the painful throb of her heart, still pounding "Perce, Perce, Perce." She only remembered the hollow thought, "I can't save him now," and someone helping Aila carry her into the house...

Shadow and fiery light... a strange tingle pulsing through her veins. She was lost, somewhere inside herself, a place she did not know. It wasn't part of her...Someone calling...

"*Phoenix.*"

She was flying, flying over Pelanca, on wings...her feathers as golden red as the city looked to her eyes. There was no darkness here...

"*Phoenix!*"

Phoenix, yes...not Shadowchild. I am Phoenix.

"Ben-nie!"

She turned. She knew that voice, more beautiful to her than Reyortsed's. She thought she'd never hear it again.

"Bennie, come down now. I need to tell you something."

Perce...

She flew down to him.

Oh, he's here! He's not dead after all!

In a wheel of fire she was Bennie again, running into his arms, sobbing with joy.

"I thought you were gone! I thought I could never get you back now!"

Perce just smiled, holding her face between his hands.

"My Bennie," was all he said, and led her into his apartment. Bennie followed, talking excitedly, pushing all the pain and fear she had been feeling aside with her words.

"We can call Aila, and let her know you're back safe. I'll go get Sean and Gemini and we can sort everything out. We were all so freaked out, Perce, you have no idea! But..." Her voice trailed off when she saw that Perce was gazing out the window with an unreadable, if thoughtful, expression. She didn't have to ask him what he was thinking. She already knew.

"You're not back safe, are you?" She said quietly, "This is just a dream, isn't it?"

"No," Perce said, barely above a whisper. "Not just a dream."

He turned to her, his face both happy and sad.

"We're not really here, as you said, but I'm not just your mind and heart refusing to deal with reality either. I did die out there, Bennie, but when I sent you the energy and transferred the power to you I left this imprint here for you to find. You need to know a lot of things, now. I was going to come and tell you the other night, but unfortunately my stupidity sidetracked me, and now this is the only way I can."

Bennie shook her head. "You shouldn't have given so much energy to me!" She stormed. "You wore yourself out and you couldn't fight off the elves or their spell! Now you're dead because I wasn't strong or fast enough!"

"No, Bennie, that's a lie," Perce said firmly, seating her on the sofa. "Reyortsed had poisoned me long before he ever contacted you. I was dead anyway, once I relinquished the power I gave to you. The elf's hex was a bluff to make you think it was your fault.

"Secondly, you had to make it out of there, not me, *you*. And with the stunt you pulled on Gregk-which was brilliant by the way, and I'm really proud of you-but with that stunt, there was no way you could have handled the power transfer. This sleep that you're in proves that. It's a strong thing, Bennie, and we need to talk about it.

"Yeah," Bennie said, blinking back tears. "I was kind of wondering why I was suddenly a bird flying around, and why it meant so much to Reyortsed to get his hands on this ability."

Perce laughed. But even though it was the same laugh that always made Bennie feel happy too, she only felt a pang when she knew this was the last time she would hear it.

"Oh Bennie, you can make a joke out of the most serious things," he said, giving her a one armed hug. He sobered up when he saw she wasn't smiling. "But it's not just a shape-shifting ability Bennie, it's far more."

"Tell me."

"Do you remember when I first told you about the Guardians, and how I spoke a bit about Reyortsed's history, and about Sheyneh?"

Bennie looked at him curiously. "Yes, I do."

"I told you about her immortal power that was passed on from heir to heir through the generations, and I remember you were curious about the tattoo on my hand that matches the mark on your shoulder."

"Perce, are you telling me what I think you are?"

"Yes Bennie, you are an heir of Sheyneh."

Bennie took this in slowly. It wasn't hard to grasp, just scary. And it added a couple hundred more questions to her growing list.

"So I'm an heir, and this power is now mine, but why would Reyortsed want it? If I remember correctly you told me only the truest heir can use it fully--"

Perce was looking at her with an alarming expression. Bennie stopped.

"Oh shit," she said. "*He's* the truest heir?"

"Let me explain that part a bit, Bennie," Perce said. "Do you remember that prophecy I recited? The one about the Wings of Scarlet claiming his abandoned throne?"

Bennie's heart was pounding nervously again.

"I remember now," she said. "He could use it fully but he chose a different life and never knew it was there for him, so the other heir comes to use it. But Perce, that can't be *me*."

Perce stroked her hair.

"I'm afraid it is you, Bennie. The tattoo on my finger meant I carried the power of Sheyneh. The actual mark in your skin means you are the wielder. Reyortsed was marked the same way, though I can't imagine what the inner void it made in him does to him."

"Inner void?"

"Bennie, when I went inside you to find your abilities and a suitable Night Name, I found part of your soul that was hollow, like a box needing to be filled. When I recognized the mark on your shoulder from my studies, I knew this empty space was reserved for the ability you'd come into. It was destined to hold the power of Sheyneh and only that. Reyortsed must have the same void inside him, and since it was never filled he was driven to learn what it was. That's how he caught on to us, fifteen years ago."

Bennie looked at him curiously. Perce was distant for a moment.

"That's how he caught on to your father and I."

Bennie's heart skipped a beat. She never really had been told about her dad and his role as a Guardian.

Caleb-your dad-was one of my best friends. He was an elemental mage-controlled wind, fire, water and earth, and I noticed that one day several years after we'd met he got a strange tattoo on his finger. When the time was right he explained he was an heir of Sheyneh and the current keeper of her power. It had been passed to him by his grandfather instead of his estranged uncle because his uncle had never been a true Guardian and was on a path in the darkness."

"So Reyortsed is my dad's uncle, and when he found out about the power he came after my dad to claim his right to the power." Bennie said, ignoring the fact she had actually wanted to kiss someone she was related to only hours earlier. But then Reyortsed wasn't a normal human by any standard, and he had been playing with her mind.

"And your father naturally fought to keep the power from the hands that would destroy us," Perce said quietly.

"We worked together as architects at our own company," Perce said. "I remember the night we were shutting down our last project, when Reyortsed showed up.

"I had gone to our portable to get some paperwork, and when I came back around to the front of the site I saw your father fighting back several serpentine creatures, the same kind that attacked you and Peter. I was able to help him get rid of them, but he was too far gone from the acid.

"He told me Reyortsed figured if he couldn't have the power, he'd stop Caleb from being able to pass it on to another heir. He knew Caleb couldn't die until someone else held the power, as it was self-protecting, but he didn't know your mother was already pregnant with you, and that his attempts had been in vain."

Bennie felt a surge of anger. She had never known her father because of the selfishness of another man, whose cause was never achieved anyway!

"I can never stop thinking about how I may have saved him that night if I had been outside with him," Perce said painfully. "Yet I think it was fated that I not be seen, though, so I could protect you. We may both have died had I not gone back for the papers.

"He made me promise to take care of you, and to be there when your time came, since he couldn't be. He entrusted me to carry the power until you were ready, and then I could give it to you, and only you."

"That's why Reyortsed needed me there last night," Bennie said. "To make you give up the power, and for me to think I could save you by giving it to him."

"Then he'd have killed you and left me to die, yes," Perce said. "He spoke the truth when he says he doesn't like killing, but he will if he thinks he must, and we were certainly a must for him.

"When your father had given the power over to me and died, I magicked the scene to look like he had been injured by a scaffolding that fell, and then I called 911. Naturally they pronounced him dead at the scene, asked me a bunch of mundane questions, and settled the issue as an accident. I tried to tell your mom the truth, but she didn't take it well at all and told me to leave her alone. I shouldn't have, as you've seen, but I did, and now she distrusts the Guardians and everything about them, when once it fascinated her."

"And now here we are," Bennie said, looking down at her feet. Perce sighed.

"He we are."

"So what do I do now?" Bennie said.

"Well, that's the key," Perce said to her. "You see, Reyortsed was born with his powers, and was never able to be taught how to use them properly and without infringing on the rights of others. He could convince even the most well-meaning teachers that he was doing no wrong, and with whatever help he got from the devil or his friends, he's made himself even more dangerous. The power he has mirrors the power of Sheyneh–aside from the fire and feathers, and he wanted the power to keep anyone from ever being able to resist him."

"So the power of Sheyneh is ultimately the power of persuasion?" Bennie said, understanding now how some girl no older than her had saved the universe some millennia before: she had simply convinced her enemies to stop.

"Exactly," Perce said. "Since you are the true heir, and the new being of Sheyneh, you are now Reyortsed's equal. His seduction and persuasive nature are neutralized by the simplicity of your being. Once you learn how to use your new powers and your old ones to their fullest, he will have a real enemy to face."

Bennie took this in, and immediately thought of how powerless she had been to resist Reyortsed in the school courtyard and even over the internet when he had IM'd her.

"No," she shook her head in a panic. "I can't do this, Perce. I'm nowhere near that powerful or that evil. I can't brainwash or hypnotize someone against their will!"

She was shaking now, getting up off the couch and backing away. Perce came to her, holding her hands in his, and looking her deep in the eye.

"You don't need to be ready right now. Time will give you all you need to learn, and as for brainwashing someone, I'd never tell you to do that. In fact, you have to promise me you'd never use the power in that way, right now."

"No problem, I promise!" Bennie said, but she was thinking "I won't use it at all."

"You don't need to force anyone into your way of thinking, Bennie," Perce said. "The power isn't a force, it's a view of the big picture- or the other picture if you keep a narrow minded view, which is Reyortsed's problem. Esla will be sure to see you get a good look at the big picture so you can know just how and why to use your abilities. You won't go wrong, Bennie. I swear."

Bennie just looked at him, not even trying not to cry now. She was so overwhelmed, and remembering that Perce wasn't going to be there with her through all these new things she had to learn. Perce seemed to know she was thinking this, but then, they were in her head, after all.

"Bennie, I wish I could be there with you when you need me, but it wasn't meant to happen. You need to not worry about me or about yourself. You're going to do great, you and Sean and Gemini, everyone. You'll all be brilliant by the time this is all settled and done."

He held her a little tighter, and his voice began to sound thinner, as if he was talking through a thick span of nothingness. "Would you do me a favor and tell everyone I said goodbye, and that I love them?"

Bennie started sobbing aloud then, but she nodded into Perce's shirt. He kissed her on the top of her head.

"That includes you, my little shadow girl."

Bennie looked up at him as he let go of her. He was the only thing that hadn't disappeared into the strange fiery light and mingled shadows again, and he was slipping away now too.

"I love you too Perce. We all do."

Perce nodded as the distance between them grew.

"Be well, Bennie, and before I forget, though I think you know…" He was shouting now, but still sounding farther and farther away…

"…Your real Night Name is Phoenix, so let yourself fly!"

He was gone, and Bennie was slipping out of the colorful new part of her soul, the void now filled, and back into the light of the real day.

Chapter Thirty-One, Aftermath

Bennie snapped awake, breathing hard. She still felt fire pulsing through her.

She jerked upright in the bed, trying to get her bearings, only Aila's soothing voice and Sean's strong arms kept her down.

"Perce," Bennie said when she found her tongue. She turned her eyes to Sean's pain-ridden face. She couldn't even look at Aila.

"You tried, Bennie," the fairy said. "You tried."

Bennie looked down at her hand, the one Perce had taken in his before her transformation.

The mark she had grown so used to seeing on his hand, on her shoulder, was there on her own.

I am Phoenix, but I have no wind beneath me to fly on. He was the wind.

Bennie's face crumpled with pain, and Sean grabbed her tightly in both arms.

"We'll be okay, Bennie," He said, but his own voice was quivering, and he shook as he held her.

Bennie tried to control herself. She had the least reason to cry, and Sean was about to break down. She had to help him.

A pair of smooth, white hands reached around Sean and Bennie together. Gemini was there, silent and still, but tears running down her flawless face still. Sean's racking sobs broke Bennie's wall and she took Aila's hand, the fairy still silent and white-faced with grief.

Bennie tried to speak, tried to tell them what Perce had asked her to in her dream, but she couldn't. Not now. Now she just needed to be there, with her family.

Family...

Mom.

Why didn't you tell me? Why didn't you say something?

Bennie cried.

* * *

Aila had gone away to report to Esla about Bennie's condition, Gemini's family had come looking for her, and she had gone quietly. Sean had fallen asleep at a single note Gemini had hummed and was curled in a chair by the bed.

But Bennie was awake. No music could give her sleep, no song could give her respite from all that had happened, all she had done.

I fell right into the trap. If I hadn't gone, someone else may have been able to rescue Perce eventually. If I hadn't gone-

"I know what you're thinking," Aila said. "And you're wrong."

Her sudden appearance made Bennie jump so hard that she slammed into the bedside table and sent a metal water cup to the ground with an abnormally loud clang. Sean merely stirred slightly and shifted position, turning his head uncertainly, like a little boy who lost site of his dad in a crowded room.

"Am I?" Bennie said, not questioning the fact that Aila probably did indeed know what she was thinking.

"If you hadn't gone for Perce," Aila's voice betrayed her pain when she said his name, "He'd have been gone forever. Reyortsed would never have let him escape, would never let you have a chance to gain the powers that are your right. Perce couldn't die as long as he had them. He'd be damned to hell while still on earth, and you'd—we'd—never stand a chance against Reyortsed.

"Perce's choice to put himself in this position was his own. Had he had his wits about him, he'd not have given the Dark King the chance to capture him, but Perce always thought with his heart, and he wanted to help Gemini's family. You can't blame yourself for thinking with your heart, Bennie. It was the right way, in this case."

Bennie turned away. She couldn't find fault with Perce, no matter what, and while Aila's words made sense, but Bennie wasn't ready to give in.

"Perce died helping me," Bennie said. "If I hadn't hit Gregk so hard I'd have had energy enough of my own to fight Reyortsed. Perce channeled his own energy into me and left himself wide open. Had he had any of his strength he may have lasted long enough to wait for the antidote to the poison Reyortsed gave him."

"Poison?" Aila said. "And he gave you energy?"

"Yeah," Bennie said. "While I was absorbing my new abilities I dreamed, and he was there. He told me the energy he sent me left the imprint of himself there for me to find so he could explain everything to me, and one of the things he said was he was poisoned."

"If the Dark King poisoned him, we probably wouldn't have found out what he used until too late," Aila said. "He'd make sure Perce had been exposed to it long before you ever got to him."

"Despite his favorite line: I don't like to kill?" Bennie remarked bitterly.

"He says he only kills people when he has to," Aila said, "In other words, he only kills people who won't do what he wants, or are a threat."

"Like me," Bennie said. "He won't get that chance. He'll pay for Perce's death first."

Aila was quiet when Bennie said that. Bennie wished she was as perceptive of Aila's thoughts and mind as Aila was of hers.

"What else did he say?" Aila finally asked. Sean murmured in his sleep, and Bennie looked at him thoughtfully.

"He said he loves you," Bennie finally said. "He loves us all."

Aila was quiet again. Bennie looked down at her hands; the mark looked strange on her finger. She preferred seeing it on a larger, stronger hand.

Another hand, much smaller, took hers. Aila looked closely at the mark.

"And did he tell you who you are?" She said, her voice hardly louder than a whisper.

"I am Phoenix," Bennie said. "I am the nemesis of Reyortsed."

Aila sighed quietly. Bennie looked into her eyes, eyes so tired and sad that Bennie was shocked to realize that Aila had most certainly known Perce better than Sean, Gemini, or herself, and was taking his loss harder than any of them.

How can I think she'd be stronger than us? Her burdens are heavier. How long has she lived in this world?

Bennie clasped her hands around Aila's, and gave her what she hoped was a strong, warm smile.

"I am Phoenix, and I'll see you smile again," Bennie said, meaning every word.

Tears ran out of Aila's eyes. She smiled and shook her head.

"You are Phoenix," she said, "But I see Perce looking out through your eyes."

Sean woke up some time later while Bennie and Aila discussed everything that had gone on in Bennie's dream, and during the fight with Reyortsed.

"What time is it?" He said, sounding like he didn't really care.

"Time," Bennie said. "Shoot! How long have I been here? My mom will have died of fright by now!"

"No, Bennie, it's ok," Aila said. "She's waiting outside for you right now."

"What?"

"I sent a friend of mine to tell her what happened, and she came right away. She's asleep on the sofa."

"She came to *Pelanca?*"

"It's not like she hasn't been here before, you know," Aila smiled. "Go on, you've rested the whole night. Sean will take you and your mom home on his way home himself."

"My mom will be spazzing out too," Sean said, still sounding apathetic.

"We let her know, too," Aila said. "No need to worry."

Sean unfolded himself painfully from the chair as Bennie slid out from under the blankets and took her coat off the back of the bed. Together they followed Aila out into the main room, where Bennie saw her mom sleeping on the couch, her small, tired frame curled up tightly to ward off the demons that haunted her past. Aila had put a knit afghan over her during the night.

Bennie's heart broke even more when she remembered the last time she had seen her mom sleeping. She'd just crept into the room after the major fight, and her mom's pillow had still been wet with tears. Now Bennie knew they weren't just because Bennie had upset her.

All the things you never told me. Now I know why you acted the way you did.

Bennie gently woke her mom up.

"Mommy," Bennie whispered. "I'm awake now, let's get you home."

Bonnie said nothing, just blinked and nodded. She took Bennie's hand, and with parting words to Aila she, Sean and Bennie headed to the tunnels that led them back to San Antonio.

Bennie stayed in her room, listening to the radio, thinking about what had happened while trying not to. It hurt so much.

She didn't go to school for a day, and then another. When her friends called her mom said she was resting and she'd call back when she woke up. But Bennie never slept the whole time she was in her room.

When her mom knocked on the door the second night after leaving Aila's, Bennie thought it was just to make her eat some more, but instead she found her mom taking her onto her lap like she did when Bennie was small.

Bennie was stiff in her mother's arms at first, but she softened into the embrace she'd forgotten since middle school. She sniffled into her mom's shirt, listening to her heartbeat. It was more soothing than any magical words the fairies could make or songs that Gemini could sing.

"Why didn't you tell me about Dad, mom?" Bennie said, tears soaking them both as her mom rocked her gently. "I mean, I know I wouldn't have believed you before becoming a Guardian, but why not after? Did you think I had stopped going to learn about my powers? I can't imagine you knowing all this and really expecting me to quit."

"I didn't expect you to," Bonnie said quietly. "I hoped you would though, every night you went out I hoped you'd come back and say 'that's it.'"

Bennie looked up at her mom in surprise.

"You knew I was going out and didn't stop me?"

Bonnie smiled and pushed her hair behind her ear so she could see Bennie's face better.

"I knew all along, baby," She admitted. "I hate to say it, but a lump of blankets in a bed is so obvious a trick it's not even a trick anymore.

"I didn't stop you because I knew it wouldn't work. You went out to practice that day five months ago with my eyes and came back with your dad's, and I knew I was in trouble. You were frustrated with me all the time as it were and I knew if I tried to stop you on such a large scale I'd lose you forever.

"That's what scared me. I don't mind the Guardians, I know they mean well, but with my husband being one, that's one thing, like he's serving in the military. I knew what he was and I chose to be with him, to risk losing him one day. With you, I didn't get a choice.

"Bennie, Perce tried to explain to me that you were a very important person to the Guardians, but neither of us got to choose ourselves, it just happened. I couldn't lose you too."

Bonnie was crying, and Bennie reached up to stroke the tears from her mother's face. Bonnie kept talking.

"And when I woke up the other morning and you weren't there, and Aila's friend showed up, I thought you were dead."

Bonnie held Bennie so tightly that Bennie worried about being able to breathe for a second. But she needn't have worried.

"But you weren't," Bonnie relaxed her grip to look into Bennie's eyes again. "Instead I hear that my little Bennie risked her life to help someone she loved, that in a single hour she had taken on not only her full power, but an old fear, and the Dark King himself."

Bennie's own eyes filled with tears.

"And you heard that she failed miserably. Perce died anyway."

"No, Bennie," her mom hugged her again. "You didn't fail. You couldn't save him, you know that. I heard that my daughter was capable of more than I ever wished for…and you know how ambitious I can be."

Bennie smiled at that. She did know. Her mother wasn't a lawyer for nothing.

"Bennie, when I went in and saw you there, sleeping, lost in some other world, when Aila told me your body was processing the new power, what had happened, and that you were going to be just fine, I never felt more proud of you. Even sleeping there you looked fearsome and powerful."

She sighed.

"I wish I could take credit for it myself, but the man who deserves it is the one I shunned. I should have thanked him. Now I can't."

It was Bennie's turn to hold her mom.

"He never wanted your thanks. He just wanted you to be happy again."

Bonnie looked at Bennie and smiled.

"I am happy, Bennie. Perce made me happy because he made you happy."

Chapter Thirty-Two, It Starts

Bennie sat in her geometry class, sighing as she flunked yet another quiz.

This just isn't my grading period. Maybe the next six weeks-

She snapped out of her thoughts again. Mr. Franks was going over the problems on the quiz. She had to figure out what she did wrong.

She looked down at her quiz. This step was right, that step was right-ahh, she'd totally skipped putting pi into the calculator when getting the area of the circle.

Too busy thinking that I should take Sean some of mom's apple pie...

The bell brought her back to reality. She stuffed her quiz into her binder and made her way to the door. Sarah would be waiting at the bus circle with Rachel. She was spending the night at their house along with Rachel's friend Cassie-

"Bennie, can I have a moment?"

Mr. Franks' voice made Bennie's stomach drop with the dead, aching weight she always got when she knew she was in trouble, or could be.

She sat down on the edge of one of the desks.

"I've been concerned about your quiz grades," Mr. Franks said. "Your homework is okay, but I'm not sure if you're not getting the idea of the work or you're just distracted by something."

Bennie fiddled with the zipper on her backpack.

"It's just distraction," she said. "I know what I'm doing, I just can't focus. The slightest thing sets my mind off these days."

"Any idea what it is?"

Bennie fiddled with the zipper some more. She didn't feel like talking, but Sarah and Rachel were waiting. She had to get this over with.

"I lost someone I loved recently," she said.

"Ah," Mr. Franks said, his tone softer. "Before school?"

"No, about a week and a half ago, actually."

Mr. Franks looked at her with the same gaze she saw in Aila's eyes.

"I think you've been distracted longer than that. You've looked lost since you first came into my classroom."

Bennie looked up at him. Now that he mentioned it, she realized she had been lost to the world since her first days as a Guardian.

"Different things, I guess," Bennie said. "I've had a lot of change going on since the summer, and losing my friend...I just don't know anymore."

"Anyone you trust advice from?"

"My dead friend," Bennie remarked, smiling mirthlessly.

Mr. Franks grinned.

"Bennie, I'm an old guy. My daughter just left for college, so I know about the trials of teenage-hood, and while I can't tell if everything you're going through is normal, I can tell you no matter what it is-guys to mascara to saving the planet-you can't go it alone. Don't be afraid to trust people, and don't be afraid to trust yourself, because half the time you already know the solution to your problem, which is, in this case, *stop worrying.* You'll make yourself sick, as well as mess up your good grades. Focus on the now, and think about the future, not the other way around."

He smiled, and Bennie felt something move on her face, a pulling... She was smiling back.

Bennie ran to the bus and plunked into the seat next to Rachel. Sarah turned around in her own seat and looked at Bennie curiously.

"Where were you?" She said. "You nearly missed the bus."

"Just asking Mr. Franks about the quiz," Bennie said, busying herself with settling her backpack on her lap while Sarah squealed when she turned around and found herself face to face with a bee.

"Oh no you don't!" She swatted it away from the soda she had bought from the library club in the bus circle. "That's mine!"

"I'll get it," one of the guys sitting across from her reached out to smash it when it settled momentarily on the seat.

"Mmm," Rachel sounded like she was about to say something, and Bennie remembered that she was considerably *closer* to bees than other humans. She wouldn't want the little thing killed.

And I've certainly had enough of killing.

"I would just leave it alone," Bennie interjected as quickly as possible. "Don't make it angry."

But the boy had already swung at the bee, and missed. The bee spun up above them and set the already loudly talking girls shrieking and the guys swatting. The poor, confused little bee buzzed straight to Rachel, and Bennie realized she wasn't biting back words, she was humming with concentration as she willed the bee to understand her.

"Don't move!" Sarah said as the bee leveled itself with Rachel's eyes. She darted her eyes to the window quickly and looked back at it. The bee hovered for a moment before flying out the window and being buffeted away by the wind the cars created.

Rachel stared after it, and Bennie put a hand on her shoulder. She was the only one who had a clue what was going on in Rachel's head.

"I just hope I didn't save her from a smashing here so she could be a bug spot on another bus' windshield," Rachel said sadly. "Poor baby. The school bees are so sweet and clueless, drunk on all that soda and so used to humans they don't know they might as well be in a nest of vipers. Why do people automatically think 'must kill' when they see them?"

"I don't know," Bennie said. "I guess since bees sting, people think they're a threat."

"And the irony is they only sting when threatened." Rachel said. "All the senseless killing, even amongst humans, simply because the other side is a "threat." It's so stupid!"

"I know," Bennie said, clenching her jaw. Senseless, and she'd lost Perce for it. She felt anger boiling inside her now, like a fire, an explosion.

It has to stop.

Rachel suddenly flinched, and Bennie jerked her hand off her shoulder. That hadn't been just a feeling. Bennie had nearly transformed right there in the school bus.

"Sorry," Bennie said, checking to make sure she hadn't burned Rachel severely. The younger girl shook her head.

"It's ok," she said. "I've been worried about you, though. You still holding up?"

Bennie looked at her hand, curled in a fist. She opened it and found a single feather, like a downy fire, sticking out of her palm.

"I keep doing that, but that's the first time I've grown a feather," Bennie said out loud. *This has to stop.*

"Doing what? Where did it come from?" Rachel watched as Bennie plucked the feather from her skin.

"I'll explain tonight," Bennie said, sending a glance toward Sarah, who was looking at a magazine full of homecoming dresses with another girl

Shadowchild

Bennie didn't know. She hadn't seen the feather or heard the conversation about the bee.

Rachel gently took the feather and examined it in silence. Bennie said nothing, but in her mind she was far from quiet.

This does have to stop. I have to stop having a reason to feel this way, to get angry enough to lose control of my powers or transform. Reyortsed has to stop.

And I seem to be the best person to stop him, if not the only one who can.

Bennie and Rachel waited until Cassie and Sarah had finally crashed on their sleeping bags about halfway through the third Ben Stiller movie Bennie had been put through. Laughing wasn't easy for Bennie right now, and she'd have rather watched something that didn't require her to be as theatrical as the actors on screen.

They got up quietly and tiptoed out to the alleyway in the backyard. There was a large bush that had more or less replaced the fence some years earlier. Bennie remembered how she and Sarah used to hide inside it for a clubhouse, and Rachel would come try to tag along. Bennie felt a little guilty about how she had gone along with Sarah and made Rachel stay outside the entrance to guard for boys just so she and Sarah could play alone.

Whether or not Rachel thought of this now, she ducked into the shrubbery, amazingly still hollowed out as it had been when Bennie was ten. Bennie followed her.

"Why did we come here?" Bennie said.

"Because it's not just a secret hideout anymore!" Rachel said. "It's my road to Pelanca!"

"What?"

"You know how the Guardians have all these entrances that only Guardians can go through, and normal people just find to be ordinary things?

237

This one apparently has been here all along and we didn't know about it because we weren't Guardians yet."

"Yeah," Bennie said. "But why here? It's hardly a public route."

"Well maybe it was meant to be here just for us!"

Bennie crawled down into the tunnel, which seemed much smaller to her now than it had five years earlier, and suddenly it grew. She could stand now, and there weren't roots under her feet, only rock.

She continued forward towards the glow coming from the cave's mouth, and there was Pelanca City, beautiful as always, but glittering under a starry night sky.

"Wow," Bennie said. "It never ceases to amaze me, but why are we here? Sarah and Cassie could wake up and see we're gone."

"Don't worry, Sarah knows more than she lets on about me." Rachel said. "She tried to follow me once but when I vanished and came back she knew I had my reasons for what I was doing. I helped her get through so she could see my reasons. She'll cover for us."

"Sarah knows you're a Guardian?"

"Yeah, sort of. She doesn't understand exactly what we are but she gets the idea that we're special. Seeing Pelanca has that affect on people. I trusted her because she's the only one who'd actually believe it if anyone in my family was told-all those Harry Potter books she reads. I didn't like them much but I think I might try them again after this."

"Does she know about me?" Bennie asked.

"No, I figured you'd tell her when you thought the time was right.

"And for your other question, we're going to Jinx's to see Gemini. She's worried about you. Sean comes by but neither of them have seen you since..." She trailed off awkwardly.

"Yeah," Bennie said, concentrating on the pathway down the slope into the city. "You'll need to lead the way, I have no clue where Jinx lives. I've only met her once or twice, after all."

"That's true," Rachel said, glad of the change of subject. "We'll have to take some public transportation. You know, big city and all."

"No it's ok," Bennie said, wondering what kind of transportation Rachel was talking about, since there appeared to be no busses or taxis. Just the occasional car-like pod that glided about silently.

"We'll just wait here for a dragon to come along--" Rachel said.

"What?" Bennie jumped. Rachel couldn't seriously mean they were going to fly on a dragon!

"I'm *kidding!*" Rachel laughed. "No, we take a transporter."

She pointed to what looked like an over-sized telephone booth. Bennie felt a pang as she remembered Perce claiming he wouldn't clutter up his apartment with the arriving half. *"Flying's more fun anyway,"* he had said.

Bennie followed Rachel into the transporter and shut the door. Rachel typed in a number on a small keypad after looking it up in a directory. "I can never remember what the number for the transporter on her street is," Rachel muttered under her breath by way of explanation.

As soon as she hit "Enter" Bennie found herself on the other side of the oversized booth. It took her a minute to realize she was actually in another transporter: the scenery outside had changed.

Explains the extra space.

She followed Rachel out the door and down the residential street to a small house that looked oddly normal for a magical city on a different plane of reality. Rachel knocked on the door, and Bennie heard an enormous crash and several voices all at once.

"I'LL GET IT!"

"I'M CLOSER!"

"WOULD YOU RELAX! I'M ALREADY UP!"

"NO! GO CLEAN THE MESS YOU MADE WITH DINNER!"

"HEY STOP SHOUTING! I'M TRYING TO WORK!"

Rachel giggled. Bennie just stared at the door in shock.

"How many people live here?" She said, looking at the small house.

"Um, a considerable number," Rachel grinned.

"How many?"

"You'll see."

The door opened and a small boy with jet black hair and pale, pale, pale blue eyes peeked around at them.

"Hi Kane," Rachel said.

"Rachel!" He said, sounding considerably older than the four-year-old he appeared to be. He let them inside and pushed the door shut, both hands on the doorknob.

"GEMINI!" He sang down the long hallway.

"Kane?" Gemini peeked around the corner, "Your mommy needs help in the kitchen." She raised her eyebrows at him and the boy ran giggling down the hallway.

Gemini turned her eyes to Bennie. They were so sad. She swiftly and gracefully closed the space between them and embraced Bennie tightly.

"You've been hiding out in San Antonio so long. I've been worried about you."

"I'm sorry," Bennie said. "Have you seen Sean at all?"

"He's here," she said. "Come on in."

Bennie followed Gemini into a house that was most certainly larger and more interesting inside than out. There were stairs going up and down and the tan, plaster walls were covered with shelves of strange contraptions, artifacts, and ornaments. Some were familiar, like the clocks and an occasional bottle or box, but others looked unusual, like the swirling blue stones.

"Eleven," Rachel whispered in Bennie's ear. "Twelve including Sean, though he doesn't live here."

Bennie bit her lip to keep from laughing. Jinx apparently had a big family.

Her good humor faded when she followed Gemini into the next room, full of books (ancient and 21st century) and found Sean, slumped up against a bookshelf, attempting to look at a page in one of the books.

"Sean," Gemini said. "Look who's here."

Sean turned his tired, dead eyes up to look at them. He came to life slightly when he saw Bennie.

"Where the hell have you been?" He said, his voice sounded out of practice, an obvious tribute to the lack of joke-making he had made recently.

He got up off the floor clumsily and came toward her. He was so pale and thin.

"Sean," Bennie felt her eyes tearing up when she saw him.

"I'm ok," He said suddenly, looking down at himself. "I've been-kinda sick."

"I can see that," Bennie said. She knew what kind of sickness Sean had. "I'm sorry."

"It's not your fault," Sean said, taking Gemini in one arm and Bennie in the other.

"Hey, I thought I heard you in here, Reyna!" Jinx came into the room, running her hand over a broken plate, the cracks shrinking each time until the plate was whole again. Her eyes moved from Rachel to Bennie. "And you brought the missing matey!"

"Hey Jinx," Rachel said. Bennie smiled at the elf.

"It's been a long time, Bennie," she said, shaking Bennie's hand. "How are you holding up?"

"Managing," Bennie said.

"Well once I fix the mess my little pal Kane made in the kitchen we'll be eating, and you're welcome to join us.

"I'd like that," Bennie said, and Jinx left with Rachel to go find the war zone in the kitchen. Bennie stood there with Sean and Gemini quietly.

"It's a bit late for dinner," Bennie said.

"We're not exactly in the central time zone," Sean remarked, some of his old grin gracing his face once more.

"True," Bennie said. "I hadn't thought of that."

They stood in awkward silence again. Bennie couldn't believe how distant she seemed from them without Perce. It felt like he was the only thing she had in common with a nineteen-year-old WOW addict and a first-rate seductive goddess. It was pathetic how little she knew of the people she spent so much time with.

He was what we had in common, and he's what we need to discuss now. Bennie thought. *That's why you're here isn't it? To talk to them?*

"Is there somewhere we could go?" Bennie said, "Somewhere private, that I could talk to you guys? What I need to tell you is pretty important."

Bennie felt her heart beginning to pound. Why was she so nervous?

"We'll go upstairs to my room," Gemini said.

The three of them hurried out of the library. Gemini went smoothly and quietly up the stairs first, and down a long hallway to a door at the end. Sean and Bennie's human footsteps seemed louder than normal behind her as they followed her through the door.

The room on the other side was remarkable to say the least. There was no ceiling, only the open sky, the walls came only halfway up, and the only furniture was a small garden table and chairs that accommodated Gemini's deron harp. The rest of the balcony-for it was more that than a room-was covered in flowerbeds, and a small tree grew over a patch of grass that Bennie assumed was where Gemini slept when she needed to.

"We goddesses like nature," Gemini smiled at Bennie's surprise. "After all, we 'made' the world that way didn't we?"

"Like you really could make Earth," Sean remarked flatly, but the banter was in his voice.

Bennie gazed out at the wonderful view of Pelanca the balcony gave her.

So peaceful...

"So what's up, Ben-jay?" Sean said, sitting down in one of the chairs as he plucked at the deron's strings absently. Gemini reached out to still the hum and gently moved his hand away from the string. She looked at Bennie.

"I think we already know, don't we?" she said. "Is this about Perce?"

Bennie looked hard at a small purple flower in the bed in front of her.

"Sort of," she said quietly as she fingered it gently. Sean shifted uncomfortably.

"Hey, I don't know if we should talk about this right now," he said. "None of us is exactly sane yet."

"It's not like that," Bennie said. "It's not just him, it's something I found out about him, and Reyortsed, and me."

That got Sean's attention. Gemini's had never faltered. Her eyes were fixed on Bennie's hands as they fiddled with the flowers.

"Bennie, where did you get that?" She pointed to the tattoo on Bennie's finger. Perce's tattoo.

"That's what I need to explain." Bennie said. "Do you know what this means? Sean and I were trying to figure it out some time ago." She held up her hand.

"Yeah, I told you I always thought it was just the product of a college night that involved one too many beers," Sean said. "How did you end up with it?"

"It's the symbol of Sheyneh," Gemini said. "I never knew why Perce had it on his hand, but I guess now it's a mark of some sort of power you pass from one person to another?"

"Yes," Bennie said. "When...when Perce and I were with Reyortsed, Perce was trying to protect me, and sent me a burst of his energy...his life force. I thought it was what- cost him his life but it wasn't- he passed on this power to me before he...and he left something of himself in me that made me dream when I got away and fell asleep. He-was *there*. It wasn't like a dream-he was really there talking to me, and he explained I was now in possession of the power of Sheyneh."

Sean and Gemini just watched her, so she kept going.

"But he said I wasn't just any old person protecting it, though," Bennie said. "I was different."

Bennie pulled back her shirt collar to reveal the pale mark on her shoulder. Sean knew about it already, but Gemini started when she saw it as what Bennie was trying to say for all her babbling sank in.

Bennie was about to continue when there was a knock on the door. Rachel put her head in.

"I was wondering where y'all went," she said, then saw Sean and Gemini's faces. "Am I interrupting anything?"

"No," Bennie said, "Actually you should hear this too, since I promised you an explanation for the feather trick on the bus."

Rachel nodded and sat on the floor against the closed door. She watched Bennie with the same rapture as the others as Bennie continued to explain her ordeal and transformation at the school, her conversation with the spirit Perce and her link to Reyortsed. She mentioned the time she spent with Aila afterwards and the talk she had with her mom and all the things that had been keeping her distracted and out of touch with them for the past weeks. It was like excavating enormous, painful stones of worry from her chest with every word.

When she finished the three of them continued to just eye her, dumbfounded. The silence was unbearable.

"Someone please say something." Bennie said, counting the seconds of quiet.

One, two, three, four...

"Holy shit," Sean finally said. It broke the hypnosis that still had Gemini and Rachel lock-eyed to Bennie.

"Sean!" Gemini said.

"Not exactly what I was looking for," Bennie said, a laugh gasping from her throat. Both Sean and Gemini let out quiet laughs themselves.

"So that's why you grew a feather in your hand today?" Rachel said.

"Yeah," Bennie said. "My real night name is Phoenix, not Shadowchild, and I have a bone to pick with Reyortsed-several in fact."

Bennie was surprised by how determined she sounded suddenly, but the anger she felt bubbling inside her wasn't a shock to her.

She remembered Sean's face when she first saw him earlier on, looking up from his book. She remembered the sadness in Aila's voice and the subdued energy in Gemini's walk. Reyortsed was responsible. He had caused that by killing Perce, and Bennie would see to it that he knew what he had done, to them and to everyone else he'd hurt.

The anger turned to heat, and then fire. Bennie jerked it into her hands before she exploded into a fiery bird again. A cluster of flaming feathers shot from her hands as she clapped them shut to stop the flames. They fell glittering to the ground and withered into nothing.

"You have to admit the feather thing could make a remarkable magic trick," Rachel said. But Bennie couldn't smile.

"There's so much anger in me," she said, wondering what would happen if she couldn't control it. "How much of it is mine and what is just a result of the power?"

"It's all yours, Bennie," Gemini said. "If any of the anger was not yours you could not control it as you just did. I know why you're angry, and you will need it to get through what lies ahead."

"And you'll need us," Sean said, putting one hand on each of her shoulders. "All of us. We're not going anywhere, and we'll be here for you."

"Well, we're going to have to finish training first anyways," Bennie said, "So where else will you be?"

"I don't know, Bennie," Sean said. "Without Perce we don't have a trainer, so we may end up being in different groups."

Bennie hadn't thought of that.

"They can't do that!" she protested. "We have to stick together!"

"It's ok, Bennie," Gemini said, "Most people don't have just one trainer and group the whole time anyway, as their powers manifest in different ways. It's like going from middle school to high school. We'll still get together, we just won't learn in the same place."

"We're not even in the same group and we're still friends," Rachel remarked.

"Yeah, and Peter and I still have loads to teach you about World of Warcraft," Sean grinned. Bennie just smiled and shook her head.

"I hate to tell you this Sean but I'd sooner go on another walk home with Peter than play World of Warcraft again."

"Why, because he's so much better than you?"

"No," Bennie said. "Because-"

"-It's an annoying, time consuming obsession!" Gemini and Rachel said in vehement unison. Bennie grinned.

"That I don't want to get into," Bennie finished.

Sean pulled on an offended look.

"Now I have no idea what you could possibly mean!" Sean said, but let it rest.

Bennie looked out at the city view again, and remembered that Reyortsed wanted control of Pelanca more than anything else in the universe. Defending such a place would be hard.

"I think we'll all have enough of war before this is over and done with," Bennie said. "With or without simulated role playing."

That quieted them a bit as they let the truth of that statement settle in.

Perce was just the first of many losses, Bennie thought. *I could lose any of these people in this house before it's all over. I want to know them better than I do now so I don't miss the chance to.*

"Maybe I'll play a game or two, just for the 'practice,' as you call it," Bennie said. Gemini and Rachel groaned as Sean cheered.

"Hurray! I've got another one addicted!"

Bennie just smiled and rolled her eyes at Gemini, who winked knowingly.

"And I'll have to find out what you spend your time doing so I can make sure you don't feel left out," Bennie said to her.

"I thought that would be obvious," Gemini said.

"I don't know," Bennie said. "I know you like music."

"Bennie, look around you!" Gemini smiled. "I like gardening."

Bennie blinked as she realized the flowers growing on the balcony had to have come from somewhere.

"No duh," Bennie laughed sheepishly. "It is obvious. You'll have to teach me though. Gardening in Texas consists of planting a couple dozen different things and seeing what survives and what doesn't."

"Not necessarily," Rachel said. "My aunt knows a thing or two about how to get things growing."

"Well the only thing that's growing right now is the coldness of dinner!" Jinx peeked her head around the door. "It's just been set out if you are ready to eat."

"I could go for something," Sean said, sounding like it was the first time in ages he'd had an appetite. Jinx smiled.

"We'll all be down in a minute," Gemini said, but Bennie was panicked.

"Wait, Rachel," she said. "How long have we been here? The others are probably freaking out by now."

"It's not been any longer than an hour," Rachel said, "But maybe we should head back, just in case."

"I'll pack you both some, then," Jinx said, running down the stairs. Bennie's friends looked at her.

"So?" Sean said. "This isn't something to shout about, but when the time comes?"

"We'll worry about it when that time arrives," Gemini said. "Now we must get some food in you."

Sean seemed perfectly happy with that arrangement. Gemini embraced Bennie again.

"Come around more often," she said in her ear. "I'll be here."

"I will," Bennie said, pulling back to give Sean a hug.

"I'll be waiting for you to show me your lycanthropic skills," Bennie said. "I'll bet a week's worth of WOW lessons that you can't get it before Christmas."

"You're on," Sean said, and raced ahead of them down the stairs to find the food.

Bennie and Rachel followed Gemini down to the kitchen where Jinx handed the two of them some paper plates loaded with exotic smelling vegetables of some sort in a meat sauce.

"This is my mom, by the way, Bennie," Jinx gestured to an elf who looked almost exactly like her, only with longer hair.

"Can you two not stay?" she said, her voice friendly.

"No, we have to get back before anyone wonders where we sleep-walked to," Rachel grinned.

"Ah yes, well, enjoy the food and do come by again! It was nice meeting you, Bennie!"

"Nice meeting you!" Bennie said as she and Rachel hurried out the door.

They got through the transporter and to the bushes behind Rachel's house and back in doors. Once they assessed no one was awake and looking for them they began eating the tasty meal they'd brought with them.

"So, about this Phoenix thing," Rachel said. "What do you think you're going to do?"

"I don't know yet," Bennie answered honestly. "I'm just trying to get my grades up in school again, and to sort out losing Perce and all."

They ate a little more in silence.

"I think you talking to them helped a bit," Rachel said. "Gemini's been so quiet and Sean just comes over and sits there with her, and you've been so distracted too. I think with us knowing what's going on now we can all focus a bit."

"I should have done it sooner, I'm sorry."

"Don't be. You needed time, but now we can focus on what's ahead."

"Yeah, and there's so much ahead," Bennie remarked to herself. "So much ahead, so much to learn, and to do."

"We can handle it," Rachel said.

"Yeah," Bennie said. "I think we can."

They threw away their plates and went upstairs to brush their teeth before joining their sleeping friends for the remaining hours until sunrise.

Shadowchild

<u>Acknowledgements</u>

If it weren't for Sean and Shannon, my siblings, I'd have never gotten the idea for this book, so thanks for being your silly selves! I love you and miss being under the same roof.

I also would like to thank Cary Clack, Mrs. Koch, Sean, and Dad for picking out my mistakes and Shanna for catching what they missed, and for making a clean and beautiful manuscript for me to print. I also want to thank Dad for putting in the finishing touches prior to publication, since I was too busy writing this page and the next book! Dad, your enthusiasm is what brought this book into the light.

I owe tons of thanks to Deborah for modeling for my cover; you're a beautiful touch to a product of my heart. And to Merrie, for helping me get the AIM formatting correct. Nathen, thanks for giving me the real life WOW experience!

I want to thank Mom for being so patient with me all this time and not committing me no matter how nuts I sounded, talking about people in my head. I also want to thank my teachers, among whom are those who suggested I try making books my career. You know who you are!

Thank you, Charlotte, for giving me the opportunity to illustrate your books. And thanks for all your advice from one writer to another. God blessed me when he put you in my life!

I want to send a shout out to all the authors whose wonderful books I have read while growing up. You are my heroes.

And last but not least, thanks to Felisha, Mark, Shannon Sams, and everyone else who read my book first and who supported me throughout the process. If I forgot your name just hit me and I'll add it next time if there's room on the page.

And most of all, thanks to God, because nothing would exist if he hadn't made it!

Bennie will be back!

About the Author:

Caera Elizabeth Thornton is a lifelong lover of literature, art and music. She spent her childhood alternating between reading and writing stories, and as a teenager took to drawing as well. She has currently illustrated two books as well as her own: Juanito de Andalucia and Antonio de Andalucia: El Rey Futuro by Charlotte Brokaw Powers. While raised most of her life in San Antonio, Thornton currently attends Baylor University in Waco, Texas, where she studies professional writing and music.

For more information, please visit
www.myspace.com/authorcethornton.